THE LAST DAY OF SCHOOL...
FOREVER

"Psst, hey Vic," I whispered. "1975. Nine-teen-seventy-five." I held up my fingers as I mouthed the numbers.

He looked at me, joining the club of confused friends at the back of the room. He and my best friend Dean shared a look.

The test was handed out shortly after.

I did my best to ignore the stares from the three next to me. If my plan had gone right, we'd all be acing this test.

I passed my test forward to the girl sitting in front of me to agrade. Taking hers, I uncapped my pen and stared down in horror.

The questions were all different.

I hadn't even noticed and just wrote down the answers I had remembered.

Somehow, the test had changed!

Books by Squall Charlson

Terror Valley
1. School's Out For Never!
2. You're Not My Sensei
3. This Way to Camp Blood
4. Fear the Frost Biters

Available from **Zetto Publishing**

A **TERROR VALLEY** NOVEL

School's Out For Never!

Squall Charlson

ZETTO **Z** PUBLISHING

School's Out For Never!

Cover Illustration by Marcelo Biott
Edited by Lauren Charlson

ISBN 978-1-964224-06-0

Published by Zetto Publishing
www.ZettoPublishing.com

For Dad.

I promised the first one
would be for you.

──── *CHAPTER 1* ────

I spent the entire night watching a back to back horror movie feature – so it was no wonder why I was asleep first thing in class the next day.

The whole class was laughing, I realized mid sleep, and *that's* what woke me up. If you've ever been woken up to someone laughing at you, you'll know how I felt. Actually, times that feeling by thirty for the whole class, and *then* maybe you'll know how I felt.

Dean Brown, my best friend, gave me a good slug in the arm; that helped jolt me awake.

"Dude, I think you were drooling," he whispered to me.

I quickly checked my shirt and saw a single damp line had run down it. Trying to be as cool as possible, I patted the front of it dry it before anyone noticed.

Our teacher, Mrs. Teagan, stood like a statue at the front of the room. Her wrinkled mouth was warped into a frown – one much worse than the one she *usually* sported.

"Mr. Shiner, I was hoping we were going to finish out the year with at least *one* day you didn't fall asleep in this classroom," she spoke, drawing more laughter from the class.

She was right. I had probably fallen asleep every day since fifth grade began this school year.

Cut me some slack.

Between school and homework, the only time left for a kid to enjoy some video games or to watch movies, was at night.

I'll be honest with you at least; I hardly

ever do my homework.

But, don't tell my parents that.

My name is Freddy Shiner, I'm eleven years old (birthday coming up in June), and today was *officially* my last day of fifth grade.

My last day of elementary school as a whole.

Finally.

It felt like it took so long.

After today, just one last day, I had three whole months of summer vacation ahead of me. I was in the clear.

Usually the last days of school are party days.

Not when you're in fifth grade apparently!

Today still seemed quiet and usual; a far cry from last year. Then, we had had not one, but two pizza parties when we finished fourth grade.

Moving into fifth grade was the worst. We didn't even get to go outside for recess anymore.

We were also doing math problems at nine a.m.

9

Can you blame me for falling asleep?

My eyes instinctively moved towards the front row, where sat Lauren Palmer. Her blonde hair was always combed so straight and perfect.

I often gazed at the back of her head from where I sat in class, but right now, she was looking *back* at me!

Her brilliant amber eyes on me turned the contents of my mouth into mush. I couldn't talk around her! Not that I ever tried...

So when Mrs. Teagan asked if I wanted to solve the problem on the board, all that came out was, "Nn–huh?"

The room laughed again.

Mrs. Teagan extended a long and bony finger, and gestured for me to join her at the front of the class.

My usual fear of public speaking was quickly amplified once I got a look at the board.

It was in another language!

How was *this* math?

I didn't know what any of this meant. There were random letters like "X" and "Y" thrown in there.

Who put the alphabet into math?

This was a joke they came up with while I was snoozing, *right?*

Mrs. Teagan's raspy voice echoed in my ears.

"If you don't solve this equation, I'm going to have to hold you back another year."

CHAPTER 2

Another year?

I gulped hard.

The numbers were floating around on the smart board now. She couldn't really hold me back, could she?

After staring silently for a few seconds, I still had no clue.

"Uhh—is it seven?" I asked.

"Which one?" She asked back.

Which one? *Which one?*

What on Earth did she mean, *which one?*

There were a few giggles in the classroom. I hoped Lauren wasn't one of them. Thankfully, I had my back to them.

I continued standing there blankly, the black expo marker extended out, but not making any progress.

I finally felt a hand on my shoulder, and nearly jumped out of my skin.

More laughs.

It was just Mrs. Teagan.

"That's alright, Freddy, take your seat." She said, returning her hands to her hips.

I kept my eyes down all the way back to my chair. I could still feel eyes on me, and it made me shudder.

"Can anyone solve the problem on the board?" Mrs. Teagan asked.

The room suddenly turned quiet.

A single hand rose up slowly.

It was Lauren's.

Mrs. Teagan handed the marker out to her as she approached the board.

Why couldn't it have been anyone else? There was no way I could pretend as if she didn't see me look like a complete loser up there.

Maybe I should have paid more attention in class.

Quickly, Lauren had solved the problem and figured out both X and Y, and even a Q I hadn't even see hidden in there. As she took her seat, her eyes and mine locked.

I quickly looked away, but I could have sworn she did the same.

Why would she have done that?

Mrs. Teagan stood next to the answer.

"I'm glad at least one of you are going to do just fine next year in middle school." Her eyes fell on me. "Some of you might want to take it easy this summer and devote time towards what we learned this year."

I heard Dean laugh, which caused me to smile too.

There was no way we were going to waste a single day on *anything* school related!

Mrs. Teagan opened her mouth to continue, but the digital clock on the wall beeped loudly to let us know it was 10 a.m.

I was *not* going to miss that next year.

The thing sounded like a storm warning, and scared me half the time. Mrs. Teagan obviously didn't know how to install it, much less turn it down. She had placed it right under another clock that had actual hands that moved, which was nice for counting down the seconds of her classes.

My homeroom class and I exited out into the hallway.

It still felt a little strange to be shuffling to different classrooms every hour, but all the teachers in fifth grade had sworn that it would help us before graduating elementary.

I still don't know how they expected us to visit our lockers, make a bathroom pit stop, refill our water bottles *and* make it to the next class, all in two minutes.

Dean's locker was right next to mine.

It was impossible to separate us.

I think the adults finally gave up and just started putting us together in everything to save time. He is my best friend, after all. Hopefully someone would send along a letter to our middle school explaining our situation.

I opened my locker and threw the math

book inside, where it thudded loudly to the bottom.

Dean stood halfway inside his own locker. He had his phone in his hand.

"Freddy, you got to see this," he said before chuckling.

I quickly looked around before sticking my head inside his locker too. On his phone was a video of a cat who had stepped through the handles of a plastic bag and got stuck. It frantically was trying to escape, but going nowhere in circles with sporadic jumps every now and then.

It was pretty funny and I laughed too.

I was very jealous of Dean in moments like this.

Why couldn't *my* parents get me a phone?

I tried to appeal to their protective nature about how I might need something in an emergency—but every year was the same story.

You're not old enough, for one.

Maybe next year.

I couldn't sneak in a tablet to school, let alone use the wifi, which was locked with a password thirty characters long. (Yeah, we tried to crack it a few times). I just wanted a phone more than anything.

I was turning back to my locker when a shadow fell over both of us.

"What do we have here, gentlemen?" came a deep and scary voice.

We both turned around, terrified.

It was our gym teacher: Coach G.

None of us knew what the G stood for.

"On our phones during school hours, I see..." Coach said before quickly snatching the phone right out of Dean's hands. "You can have this at the end of the day, Mr. Brown."

I backed away trying to look as small as I could while shutting my locker door. Before I was out of arm's length, a hand grabbed me by the collar of my shirt.

"Where do you think *you're* going, Mr. Shiner?" His breath smelled of cinnamon candies that he loved to eat. The sunglasses he wore made my face this close up look like I was staring into a fun house mirror. Also, who wore sunglasses *inside*?

"I–uhh–" I stammered.

"You and Mr. Brown are staying right here

17

until you give me... one hundred pushups."
He replied, a smile growing across his face.

CHAPTER 3

My arms wanted to scream, and I was only on pushup number four! Not to mention my fingers had found the stickiest part of the floor. From this low level, I could see where the janitors were really cutting corners.

A few kids stopped to stare down at us, but Coach barked at them to keep moving, or else they'd be joining us.

Blood pounded in my ears.

I felt lightheaded and I hadn't even hit

double digits yet.

Dean, on the other side of Coach, looked just fine. He was steadily keeping a rhythm and counting under his breath.

"14–15–16."

Coach turned to look down at me.

"Are you *shaking*, Mr Shiner? Are you *cold?* Should we call you *Mr. Shiver* instead?"

I couldn't respond, let alone breathe.

He must gotten tired of watching us because before I knew it, he hoisted Dean and I up.

"Get to class," he growled, pointing over his shoulder.

Dean snatched up his bag and together we quickly scurried away from Coach G in the opposite direction.

"I'll see you both next period!" He called after us.

I could have swore he laughed, too.

I didn't want to think about what special types of torture were in store for us, right now I had another nightmare: history class.

CHAPTER 4

There was also a pop quiz.

On the last day of school.

Who does that?!

History class was usually fun. We had one of those hip, young teachers that tried too hard to be cool rather than a teacher. It was also the only class our whole group of friends had together.

Dean, Aaron, Vic, and I snatched up the back row of seats on day one, and we goofed off back there the rest of the year.

All of our faces dropped when Mr. Meyer started handing the front row papers to pass back.

"I know what you're thinking, and it wasn't my call," he held up the remaining stack of sheets to show everyone. "Since it's my first year, they want to see how much I was able to teach in my classes. Don't worry, this doesn't affect anything on your end in this class!"

The whole room seemed to breathe a large sigh of relief together.

The girl in front of me handled back the last sheet from the pile. It was printed front and back with questions and blank lines for answers.

The four of us exchanged looks, and went to work filling out the test.

It didn't go well.

Our group exchanged papers with the people in front of us, and graded their papers while they looked over ours. The girl in front of me got a good amount correct, but after hearing each correct answer, I knew I wouldn't be in the same boat.

0/10.

I didn't get even one right.

At the top of the paper where it asked for a name was a big question mark in red ink.

I forgot to even put my name on it.

Glad it didn't affect my grade, at least.

We passed the papers forward for Mr. Meyer to collect.

"What did you get?" Aaron asked us.

Dean held up five fingers.

Vic looked smug. He held up nine.

They all turned to me. I didn't have to tell them, they already knew and couldn't keep the smiles off their faces.

I held up a big fat zero.

I was ready for summer.

——CHAPTER 5——

Gym class wasn't as bad as Coach G had led
us to believe.

He had us spread out across the gym floor,
cleaning out the equipment room, inventory-
ing what would work next year and what was
broken and had to be replaced.

It was tedious.

I'm also very sure he had *all* of his classes
today doing the same thing.

But, it was better than anything horrible I

was thinking might happen.

The hour dragged on until finally Coach blew his whistle and started clapping his hands at us.

"Alright, leave what you were working on for the next group. Get going, get going!"

I was first one out the door.

You didn't have to tell me twice.

I always managed to get to the cafeteria first. I would cut through the theater stage that split the gym and lunch room in half. But today I found it *packed* with various items from other plays over the years.

There were even castle pieces I had helped make last year here, too. It was kind of neat seeing all of it here. I fought my way through the thick black curtain to get to the other side. This alone made me feel tired.

I wasn't the biggest fan of gym class, and if I had been, this wouldn't have been too much of an issue.

I finally made my way out; my stomach was already noisily letting me know how dumb I was for skipping breakfast this morning. I never really liked eating in the morning, it usually made me feel sluggish, or even sick.

Dad as the same way. However, my mom and older sister, Julie, were the exact opposite. They would some days wake up early to prepare an entire smorgasbord of different dishes.

The smell made me want to crawl back *into* bed.

This morning they had made *four* different types of eggs. Scrambled, omelette, hard boiled, and the type that runs when you cut into it.

I skipped.

Lunch, next to art class, was my favorite time at school, and the Briarwood Elementary lunch ladies really brought it each and every day. They really knew how to cook!

I overheard a tall girl whispering something as I scooped up a tray. "... Yeah, I guess it's a new special dish?"

"Gross," her friend said and they both turned away from the line.

I should have too, but I wasn't fast enough. The lead lady had already seen me.

"Freddy! Care to try my new special dish?" She shouted and raised her gleaming metallic scoop.

In front of her was what looked like road-kill and my grandpa's arm skin, combined into one.

And it was dripping blood!

CHAPTER 6

I sat staring at the dish on my tray. It smelled sour, and I was really regretting not grabbing at least one hard boiled egg this morning.

The meat sat swimming in a pool of watered down ketchup, daring me to try it.

Aaron and Vic sat down across from me. They had the same mountain of mystery meat heaped on their tray, too.

"Apparently, it's meatloaf," Aaron said.

He took a sniff and immediately scrunched

up his face.

Vic was a little braver than us, he fished out a small portion with his plastic spork. We all watched with wide eyes as he raised it to his lips and took a bite.

He chewed on it slowly. His face danced between disgust and actual enjoyment. Finally, with a small swallow, he brightened up.

"Hey, that's actually pretty good!" He exclaimed, taking another, bigger bite this time.

Aaron and I shared the same thought. We both slid our trays towards Vic, who seemed happy to have three times the meatloaf now.

Dean jumped into the seat next to me and pulled a sandwich from his lunchbox. At the sight of the mountains of meatloaf, he coughed.

"You can't seriously be eating that, Vic."

"Mmh–it's–nmh–not that–bad!" He responded between bites.

I looked around the lunch room. Many others with similar looking trays sat staring down at them, as if they would come alive and try to crawl off the table.

Vic had already moved onto my tray of

food. I couldn't even look at the stuff without feeling queasy.

"This ketchup is really good, too!" Vic blurted out.

It was so watered down looking, it hardly resembled ketchup anymore.

"Man, I need to see if I can get the recipe to this–" Vic started saying as he stood up, but froze.

His body started shaking as we all stared on in horror.

The meatloaf, it WAS dangerous! It was killing Vic!

He rushed towards the corner of the cafeteria and doubled over the top of a garbage can. Vic let out a loud retch as the tray and a half of meatloaf came flying back up.

Everyone stared on in shock.

If there was any doubt in whether or not this stuff was edible, Vic was the proof.

"Good thing my mom always packs my lunch," Dean said smugly.

I wanted to deck the guy right then and there, but in a best-friend-way, of course.

Art class was canceled.

First lunch, and now art class. Today was just *not* my day.

Mrs. Teagan came to retrieve us all standing in the hallway in front of the dark and locked room. I was really bummed. My favorite class was art, and the teacher, Ms. Blithe, was really kind to me.

I had an aptitude for drawing.

I would scribble doodles away all day long if I could.

Ms. Blithe was the only teacher who encouraged that.

She taught us about the two hemispheres of our brain. One side, the left side, was all about reason, facts, and numbers. The right side, emotion and art. These two hemispheres control the opposite side of our bodies, so it made sense why I was always drawing; I was left handed.

Maybe I could blame my other school work on that too.

The whole class shuffled back into Mrs. Teagan's room. The hour after lunch was usually her planning hour, away from students. She didn't look too happy to be sitting in a classroom filled with them again.

"Can't believe the *nerve* of some people..." She muttered under her breath as we took our seats.

Lauren raised her hand.

My attention snapped to her.

"Mrs. Teagan, why wasn't Ms. Blithe in her classroom?" She asked.

Mrs. Teagan laughed out loud and shook her head. "That's what we all would like to know. Class, take out your final book study sheets and make sure they're complete before the end of the hour."

I found mine crumpled up at the bottom of my bag and fished it out. Holding both ends and trying to smooth it out did little to no effect.

Not that it mattered much. It was still blank.

I quickly put my name at the top at least.

How long had these been assigned?

A month now?

We had a stack of books we worked through this year, and all of them bored me to tears. I only had to read the titles on the covers to know I wanted nothing to do with them.

I did what I always would do.

Doodle.

There was plenty of room on my book study sheet.

I drew monsters with tentacles that wrapped around the edge of the page. Slime dripped from the ends of their feelers. After adding in some shading, I had to admit, it looked pretty good.

I flashed it to Dean who silently nodded his approval.

Admiring my work a little more, I stood up and stretched. Guess I didn't realize I hadn't moved much, and my leg felt slightly limp as it woke up.

"Where do you think you're going, Mr Shiner?" Mrs. Teagan asked, not even looking up from her work laid out over her desk.

"Bathroom?" I asked. A few eyes peeked at me over their books.

Mrs. Teagan set down her pen and looked up at the two clocks.

"I would if I could, but we have an assembly in a few minutes. Alright class, pack your stuff up, this assembly should take us through the rest of the day."

I sat back down.

I really *did* have to go.

I felt like my bladder could burst before this assembly was over.

——— Chapter 7 ———

"To all our departing fifth graders, good luck next year in middle school! You all really lit a fire at this school, and you should all be proud of yourselves!" Our principal spoke into a microphone.

The applause he received was lackluster.

For the thirty minutes, Principal Ong had droned on about the school and what they were going to do next year.

Who cared?

We were graduating.

After today I wouldn't have to see this place again.

The clock positioned in the gym read 2:30 p.m.

I was *so* close.

"Thank you all, please return to your classrooms, and have a great summer break!"

Again, minimal reaction. People just wanted to be done.

I cleaned out my locker pretty quickly. The handful of papers that had accumulated at the bottom all ended up in the trash. I took my bag out for the last time and felt a sudden wave of nostalgia. That's when you feel sad or overcome by something that used to be, or was. Staring into my empty locker gave me that.

I wouldn't *ever* be here again.

Leave it to me to finally understand with only ten minutes left in the school year.

I shut it for the last time.

Mrs. Teagan was handing out sheets of papers to everyone. I took one from her as she cleared her throat.

"Well, here we are kids. Another year is gone. I'm going to miss you, but I don't feel half as bad when I know that the middle school teachers will have to deal with you now!" She laughed at her own joke. "In your hands, I want you to write a message to the fifth grader who will get your locker next year."

I looked down at the paper in my hand.

What did *I* have to say to them?

I crumpled it up and threw it in the trash.

After relieving myself in the bathroom and washing my hands, I navigated the crowded hallways. Teachers stood twice as tall as the wave of kids rushed past and towards the door.

I would have moved faster, but I was at the mercy of the crowd. They pushed forward, and I moved too. They stopped, and I felt a slight crushing sensation in the process.

The clock read 2:59 p.m. above the fire alarm.

My eyes felt blinded momentarily.

Someone at the front decided to open the doors early, and the light from outside was intense. I put a hand up to shield my eyes, but I was more preoccupied with the sudden lurch forward.

Kids scrambled, cheering and screaming while shoving to make it out.

Somewhere, I heard a teacher yell.

I felt the bodies around me squeeze together. Squeezing *me* in the process.

It actually kind of hurt.

I started panicking when I couldn't take a full breath in. My lungs were so compacted that I *couldn't breathe!*

I gasped for air.

Nothing.

The edges of my world started to darken and I felt the sensation I was falling, even though I knew I was still standing.

Sometime before the lights fully flickered out, I heard the school bell ring.

It was so loud.

Had it always been that loud?

Maybe I was standing right underneath the bell? It was just so loud!

The crowd lurched forward, and I slipped below them, into the darkness.

If only I could have stayed there—things would have been *much* better.

My nightmare had only just begun.

CHAPTER 8

The whole class was laughing I realized mid sleep, and *that's* what woke me up.

Dean Brown gave me a good slug in the arm, that helped jolt me awake.

"Dude, I think you were drooling," he whispered to me.

I quickly checked my shirt and saw a single damp line had run down it. Trying to be as cool as possible, I patted the front of it dry it before anyone noticed.

Mrs. Teagan, stood like a statue at the front of the room. Her wrinkled mouth was warped into a frown again.

Again?

The word danced around in my head, I didn't know what it meant.

"Mr. Shiner, I was hoping we were going to finish out the year with at least *one* day you didn't fall asleep in this classroom," she spoke, the class laughing once again.

I was disoriented still, but didn't she say that *yesterday* to me?

Yesterday.

But yesterday was the last day of school... *right?*

I was having the worst case of deja vu.

My eyes moved towards the front row, where sat Lauren Palmer.

She was looking back at me!

Mrs. Teagan asked if I wanted to solve the problem on the board, and all that came out was, "Sure?"

The room laughed again.

Mrs. Teagan extended her long bony finger and gestured for me to join her at the front of the class.

I had nightmares about this sort of thing. Here I was standing in front of the whole class, staring at a problem that wasn't even decipherable. It was in another language!

I didn't know what any of this meant. There were random letters like "X" and "Y" thrown in there.

Then I noticed there was also a "Q" too.

Mrs. Teagan's raspy voice echoed in my ears.

"If you don't solve this equation, I'm going to have to hold you back another year."

That's when it clicked.

I looked up at the clocks over my head. Both read what I was fearing the most.

9:55 a.m.

This didn't happen *yesterday.*

It was happening all over again, *today.*

Somehow, my day was on repeat!

CHAPTER 9

Once again, I wasn't able to solve the equation.

Lauren did.

I sat stunned in my seat and didn't even notice if she again looked my way.

"I'm glad at least one of you is going to do just fine next year in middle school. Some of you might want to take it easy this summer and devote time towards what we learned this year." Mrs. Teagan said.

I heard Dean laugh.

I was too deep in my own thoughts to remember what I found funny about that in the first place.

Mrs. Teagan opened her mouth to continue, but the digital clock on the wall beeped loudly to let us know it was 10 a.m.

I scrambled out of the classroom, pushing past a few people in the process.

The hallway was filled with other fifth graders in transition. They made their stops at their lockers, or gathered in a line at the water fountain. We had one of those cool water bottle taps that filled it up easily by placing a bottle or cup underneath. It still took just as long as someone using the fountain.

I opened my locker and realized I had left my math book back in the classroom.

I was out of it.

I just wanted to crawl into the locker and hide myself away.

There was no way this was happening, right?

I've heard of extreme deja vu cases, and maybe that's what I was experiencing.

Dean opened his locker next to mine. He leaned around the open door and gave me a judgmental look. "What's your problem today, Freddy?"

I must have had a wild look in my eye because when I turned to look at him, he jumped a little.

"Nightmares or something, man?" He asked.

"Y–yeah, I would say so." I said.

Repeating the last day of school before summer break sounded like one of the worst things anyone could muster up for a nightmare.

Dean dug out his phone from his backpack. He tapped around a few times on it and laughed.

"C'mere and look at this," he gestured for me to look in his locker.

"Is it that video of a cat? Hah, you showed that to me–yesterday..." I started, but knew that wasn't right.

On his phone was the video of a cat and a plastic bag.

How did I already know what was on his

phone *before* he showed me?

Dean looked confused and a little nervous.

We stood there for a few seconds, just staring at each other. In the six years I had known him, nothing like this had ever happened. I think it scared him just as much as it was scaring me.

A large shadow rose over us.

"What do we have here, gentlemen?" came a deep and scary voice.

We both turned to see our gym teacher: Coach G.

"On our phones during school hours, I see..." Coach said before quickly snatching the phone right out of Dean's hand again. "You can have this at the end of the day, Mr. Brown."

My mouth fell open.

He turned to look at me.

"What seems to be the issue, Mr. Shiner?" He breathed. His breath still smelled of cinnamon.

"I–uhh–" I stammered.

"You and Mr. Brown are staying right here until you give me..." Coach had a smile growing on his face.

"One hundred pushups?" I cut in.

The smile on his face vanished and his mouth replaced it by dropping wide open.

"How—No—I was going to say one hundred... sit ups!"

Dean groaned. I don't know why, but I pushed it.

"No, you weren't. You were going to force us to do push ups." I protested. I don't know why it mattered. Sometimes I just liked being difficult.

"And so what if I was, Mr. Shiner?"

I looked at myself in the reflection of his sunglasses. Seriously, who wears those inside?

I didn't know what to say.

Coach did.

"Mr. Brown. Hurry on to class and tell your teacher—what's his name?"

"Mr. Meyer?" Dean responded.

"Yeah, him. Tell him that your little friend here is going to be late to class."

Dean scooped his bag out of his locker and quickly shut it before turning away. He didn't even look back, just kept walking.

I probably would have, too, if it meant getting out of trouble with Coach.

Coach turned his face back to me after making sure Dean was out of earshot.

"This is usually my free hour, but I want to see those sit-ups *AND* those pushups, too."

My mouth fell open even wider than Coach's had.

"That's right, Mr. Shiner. I want to see one hundred of each!"

CHAPTER 10

Coach wasn't kidding.

He wanted one hundred.

I got close.

My stomach hurt so bad after crunch number twenty I thought I was going to pass out.

He yelled for me to switch to pushups whenever I got too tired. As you can imagine, I was swapping back and forth between the two all hour.

At least I had a clean floor here in the gym.

After sit-up number forty and push-up number twenty five, he knew he wasn't getting more out of me and walked away.

Dying on the floor, in between sharp breaths I asked: "Can I go now?"

"Get out of here." He yelled back, shutting the door to his office on the other side of the gym. He shut it so hard, the scoreboard that hung from the center of the ceiling shook violently.

By the time I got back to history class, I had arrived mid-way through the test.

"Ah, Freddy!" Mr. Meyer had called out. He grabbed a piece of paper and met me at my desk. "We're doing a *fun* little pop quiz. Don't worry, no grades on this one, just do your best!"

He clapped me on the back, which was still very sore, and returned to his desk.

I looked down at the same questions.

At least I thought they were the same questions.

I still felt like I was taking stabs in the dark with each answer until the last one.

I *somehow* knew the answer.

I wasn't sure if it was because I really knew it, or just remembered from before. I circled the right answer and flipped it over.

Again, I had forgotten my name.

I quickly fixed that before we swapped papers.

When I got my own back, I was happy to see I actually managed a 1 out of 10 this time around.

We passed the papers forward for Mr. Meyer to collect.

"What did you get?" Aaron asked.

Dean held up five fingers.

Vic still looked smug. He held up nine.

They all turned to me.

Looking even happier than Vic's nine, I held up a single finger. They laughed again.

Yeah, it was only one correct answer. But it made me feel good.

Real good.

That was until gym class.

Even the minimal moving and counting inventory felt impossible. I was glad we weren't running around at least.

I tried to stay seated as much as I could

during the hour. Luckily, Coach didn't notice or didn't care.

I think even he knew he went a little too far and was letting me recover. My stomach growled loudly. I could not wait for lunch time. After all, it is my favorite.

I had completely forgotten about the horrors waiting for me at lunch. Before I could object, the disgusting dish was heaped onto my tray.

I grabbed a small bag of chips this time.

At least I could eat *something*.

"Apparently, it's meatloaf," Aaron said sitting down across from me with Vic.

Aaron took a sniff and immediately scrunched up his face. I didn't have to get that close. The sour odor was easy to smell across the whole cafeteria.

Vic fished out a small section with his plastic spork. Aaron looked on with shocked surprise as Vic raised it to his lips and took a bite.

He chewed on it slowly. His face danced between disgust and actual enjoyment. Once again, with a small swallow, he brightened up.

"Hey, that's actually pretty good!" He exclaimed, taking another, bigger bite this time.

Aaron slid his tray towards his friend. I was going to do the same thing, but I stopped.

Dean jumped into the seat next to me, and pulled a sandwich from his lunchbox.

"You can't seriously be eating that, Vic."

"Mmh–it's–nmh–not that–bad!" He responded between bites.

"What's the matter, Freddy? Not eating?" Dean called to me, drawing laughs from Aaron.

I shook my head.

Even though I had grabbed the chips, the sight of the lunch meat made me feel queasy. Vic had already moved onto Aaron's tray of food. I couldn't even *look* at the stuff.

"This ketchup is really good, too!" Vic blurted out.

That's when I remembered.

"Hey, Vic, you might want to slow down there..." I said to him, trying to sound as calm as possible.

"What, why? Man, I need to see if I can get the recipe to this–" Vic started saying as he stood up, but froze.

His body started shaking.

Vic rushed towards the garbage cans again. I wished I had remembered sooner and stopped him from eating so much.

Art was once again canceled.

I tried the door this time. It was locked.

We all stood outside of the dark room for a few minutes until we were retrieved by Mrs. Teagan, who was not happy in the slightest, yet again. She kept whispering one-sided arguments under her breath.

"Can't believe the *nerve* of some people..."

She shut the door behind us, and everyone took a seat.

Lauren had her hand up once again by the time I sat down.

"Mrs. Teagan, why wasn't Ms. Blithe in her classroom?" She asked.

Mrs. Teagan laughed out loud and shook her head. "That's what we all would like to know. Class, take out your final book study sheets and make sure they're complete before the end of the hour."

This was too much for me, I *had* to get

away.

I stood up, and moved towards the door.

I grabbed the plastic bookmark shaped hall pass that hung there. Mrs. Teagan looked up from her planner sprawled out on her desk, and gave me a funny look.

"Don't take too long, Mr. Shiner. Don't want you falling asleep in there."

A few of the kids chuckled, and Mrs. Teagan hastily shushed them.

The empty hallways always felt a little scary. The white speckled vinyl flooring squeaked and echoed with each step I took.

The bathroom was all the way back by the art room, and was one of those walk-in ones without a door.

Luckily the *stalls* still had doors.

Even from the last stall, I could still hear every noise that happened in the hallway. So when someone tried to open the door to the art room, and found it locked, I heard the door shake in its frame.

I even heard every word they said.

"You think you can *hide* from me? I'll figure out *which one* you are." The voice didn't sound human at first. It was high pitched and terrifying.

There was a noise I couldn't quite hear coming from out in the hall. I craned my head to hear better, but the hall pass that was resting on the toilet paper dispenser must have got caught on my jacket. It snagged and fell to the floor, the plastic noisily rolling away from my stall.

I froze.

I didn't dare even breathe.

Then I head the steps of someone walking *into* the bathroom.

"Come out, come out!" The voice said, laughing wickedly and loudly.

——CHAPTER 11——

I clamped both hands over my mouth.

I shouldn't have been as scared as I was; it was probably just Dean or Aaron playing a joke on me.

The footsteps shuffled closer.

I was in the far stall. There were only three in the boys' bathroom.

Sniff. Sniff. Sniff.

Was this person *sniffing* the bathroom?

Gross when you think about it—but they

were.

The sounds drew closer to the back where I sat as still as I possibly could. I didn't even try to twist to see through the crack near the hinges better.

I was *that* scared.

BAM!

Suddenly, the door to the first stall was kicked open.

The entire row of plastic dividers and doors shook with the impact.

A low growl was humming now, and I heard the feet shuffle closer still.

BAM!

The door next to me got the same treatment and flew open. My own stall door's tiny little metal latch threatened to unlatch even as it swayed.

I saw the shadow of the person cast along the tile floor in front of the stall.

The person was directly in front of me now!

My hands were sweating over my mouth, I didn't even dare blink. When did I last take a breath? The bathroom seemed to be spinning slightly.

The sniffing started again.

They were smelling the stall I was in!

Any moment now the door was going to be kicked in and I would come face to face with whatever this was.

But I didn't. At least not then.

My heartbeat was so loud in my ears, it helped me realize that too much time had passed. The constant frantic metronome in my body was relentless, but still—nothing happened.

I heard voices, many of them, coming from the hallways.

It was the third graders coming from lunch!

Their voices were loud and excited as they poured out into the hallway. A few came into the bathroom, laughing and making fart noises.

"A hall pass?" One of the boys said, and I heard them scoop up the plastic pass off the floor.

My stall door jiggled as another boy tried to open it up. This knocked me out of my daze and I quickly pulled myself together.

I spun around and flushed the toilet without even having used it, before throwing the door open and running out of the stall. The boys all jumped back. I was about a head or two taller than them.

Without saying a word, I snatched the hall pass from the smallest one who was holding it up.

I ran out into the hallway, and many smaller faces turned to look at me. The majority were lined up along the lockers; some were getting drinks at the fountain.

They seemed to be moving *much* faster than the fifth graders.

I spun around looking up and down the hallway for any clue as to who or what was trying to *sniff* me out.

I saw nothing.

I turned to the art room. The lights were still off inside.

What did this person want with the art room, and who were they after or hoping to find?

I wanted nothing more than to never find out; just put this all behind me and actually *start* my summer vacation.

Little did I know then that this person was looking for *me*.

CHAPTER 12

"To all our departing fifth graders, good luck next year in middle school! You all really lit a fire at this school, and you should all be proud of yourselves!" Our principal spoke again into a microphone.

Applause was still lackluster.

One of the third graders from the bathroom had his head turned and was staring at me. I tried to ignore him.

The clock positioned in the gym read 2:30

p.m.

I was so close.

I just wanted this strange deja vu day to end.

"Thank you all! Please return to your classrooms, and have a great summer break!"

I was the first one to file out, even before he had finished.

Again, I cleaned out my locker and tossed the paper pile that littered the bottom into the trash without a second glance.

I don't know why I didn't just pitch my backpack into the trash, too. I was probably going to get a new one for next year, anyway. I took it with me out of habit.

Even though I still had a few minutes before the end of day, I made my way to the front of the school. A tremor flashed through my mind of last time and nearly being squished.

I stood off to the side–*safely* this time.

The halls quickly filled up with younger grades of kids, eager to go home themselves.

I could see the rest of my class, including Vic and Dean, towards the middle. Standing just a few feet off to the side of them, was Lauren.

The clock above them read 2:59 p.m.

The door was opening down the hall and kids were flooding out. I wasn't close enough to see who had triggered the rush, but they were out and probably halfway home already.

Again, the massive push of students caught those in the hallway.

The teacher next to me shouted for everyone to calm down.

I stared on in horror. It was happening all over again. Everything from yesterday *had* repeated! That's when I looked back towards Dean and Vic.

They had managed to move to the edge of the hall, and looked to be out of the immediate pinch next to the school's trophy case.

That's when I saw a hand in the air. It had a lavender bracelet on the wrist.

Lauren had one of those.

I looked around frantically where I had last seen her and couldn't find her. That had to have been her! But now she was being trampled by the packed hallway of kids!

Without thinking, I rushed into the wave of bodies. I pushed my way through and around screaming faces, trying desperately to reach Lauren—to save her.

This was a nightmare.

Her hand fell lower, but I was still too far away.

I yelled and started lifting my legs in combination with my arms, crawling over others now.

The hand reemerged—I was right there!

I reached out towards her.

Our fingers danced just inches apart.

I yelled her name, "LAUREN!"

The bell rang its 3 p.m. shrill cry.

It was so loud it made my eyes roll up inside my head.

I wasn't going to be able to save Lauren, I realized.

My whole head felt like it was going to burst!

Something much worse was in store for me.

I screamed out her name again and again as I fell into darkness.

CHAPTER 13

"LAUREN!" I burst out screaming, rock-
ing myself forward and off balance in
my desk chair.

I fell to the floor.

Hard.

I couldn't tell if the others around me
were already laughing, or if the screaming had made them start all over again.

"Mr. Shiner!" I heard my homeroom
teacher shouting. She pushed through the

crowd that had stood to look down at me.

Her face was pale and she looked mortified. She was holding a hand to her chest, and was trying to still push through.

I sat there panting. I had sweat through my shirt, and my head was pulsating painfully.

"Dude, what happened?" I heard my best friend ask.

Turning to look at Dean, he had a mixture of laughter *and* disgust on his face.

"Wha—what happened?" Was all I could say.

Mrs. Teagan was over me now. She pushed the others back again. "Give him some room, back in your seats!"

My classmates dispersed, although their attention never left me.

Mrs. Teagan started fanning me with her free hand.

I'll say it *did* feel nice. I was burning up!

"Can you stand, Freddy?" She asked me, her eyes were wide and nervous.

"Yeah, I think so," I replied.

I tried getting to my feet, and she had to end up helping me find my balance. My head spun and I felt like I was going to pass out.

Mrs. Teagan pointed to something at the front of the room and said, "Lauren, bring that over for Freddy."

If it didn't hurt so much to open my eyes in that moment, I would have seen Lauren fetch Mrs. Teagan's office chair.

It had wheels, and arm rests on it. It was her pride and joy. All I knew was moments later I was lowered slowly down into it.

Mrs. Teagan wheeled me down the hallway in her chair. One of the wheels was in major need of grease or something, because it kept getting caught and sending me momentarily off course.

She pushed me to the front office, where a familiar door was off to the side. This room happened to be one I visited more frequently than any other kid in the history of the school.

The nurse's office.

Most the time when I visited, I was perfectly fine–I just wanted out of class, or to go home early.

Nurse Green and I played this game together for years. She sometimes would let me win and spend the rest of the hour on one of the beds.

"I'll be right back," Mrs. Teagan said to me, giving my shoulders a firm squeeze. The sensation made it hard to breathe. I felt for a moment I was back in the hallway a few minutes ago. Or I guess in a few hours to come?

This was confusing.

Mrs. Teagan opened the door and went in to talk with Nurse Green.

My head had started to clear, but the gravity of what was happening to me was beginning to really sink in.

My day was *actually* repeating. Not just crazy deja vu, or like that one movie I saw a few months ago where the main characters had to escape death after a horrible accident; this was really happening all over again.

But *why?*

I made my mind up pretty quickly that I didn't want to find out.

Did that person in the bathroom have something to do with it?

I lifted myself out of the chair and moved towards the front doors.

Mrs. Teagan and Nurse Green had come out into the hall only moments later, and one of them called to me. My head was still feeling funny, and I wasn't sure which one it was.

"Where are you going? We need you to come back!"

I knew they would be coming after me.

I moved faster.

Rounding the corner, the wall of doors appeared. They were all shut, but having left out of them a few times in the past before school was over, they were never locked from the inside.

I was right!

The first one I pushed on opened right up.

I was turned around, looking back down the hall, when Mrs. Teagan appeared first.

"Mr. Shiner, you can't leave just yet! Don't go through that door!" She yelled after me.

I only lived about four blocks away. I was ending my day early. Who cared about the consequences?

I wished I had been looking before I stepped.

Instead of the concrete platform above the

stairs outside, my foot fell through *nothing*.

I lost my balance and fell through the doorway.

My hands grabbed onto the handles of the door, and I hung there, dangling above a complete void.

I looked down and saw nothing. Pure darkness.

I let out a scream.

I wanted to swing back inside the school at least, but I wasn't strong enough and I was slipping. It happened all so quickly.

I was falling.

Falling into darkness.

Falling *deeper* into my nightmare.

I blinked, and suddenly the classroom was staring at me again. Many were laughing— even Dean next to me.

"Dude, I think you were drooling," he whispered to me.

I looked down again, checking my shirt. I zipped my jacket over it instead.

"Mr. Shiner, I was hoping we were going to finish out the year with at least *one* day you didn't fall asleep in this classroom," she

71

spoke, drawing attention away from me.

I stood up, my legs still felt weak.

I had a falling sensation with the slightest movement.

"I... " I started to say, but didn't know where I was going with it.

Instead, I got up and moved towards the door, throwing it open and walking out.

Mrs. Teagan's voice cried after me, "Come back here, Mr. Shiner! You better be headed to the front office! I'm calling them right now!"

I *was* headed toward the front office alright.

I walked up to the same row of doors.

I chose a different one this time—not like it mattered.

Gently pushing it open, what I saw chilled the very blood in my veins. It wasn't the outside as it normally was—it was darkness.

Absolutely *nothing*.

The door swung back and closed.

I was stuck *in* school, repeating this day over and over again.

CHAPTER 14

I woke up with Nurse Green standing over me. Her wide face broke into a smile.

"Feel a bit cooler now, Freddy?" she said, swiping something away on her tablet.

There was a cold compress laid across my forehead.

Everything came rushing back to me.

The reality of what I was experiencing was unheard of. What kind of sick joke would see me repeat the day right before summer vacation?

I was the only occupant of one of the few lumpy beds that lined the wall.

"What day is it?" I asked. I wasn't sure why, but I already knew the answer.

She gave me a curious look, her eyes narrowing. "Your last day of fifth grade. You don't want to waste it in here with me, do you?"

She slid backwards in her chair, placing her tablet onto the desk before wheeling with precision back over to me. Her hands reached out and took my face in them. She stared into both of my eyes, one at a time.

"Here I thought you'd *finally* figured out the best way to fake illness on the last day of school."

What I wouldn't give to have that be true. Only once in my school days had I ever been so sick I had to be taken home early. Dad came to pick me up on his lunch break, and...

That was it!

I could get my parents to come get me, and save me from this mess!

"I'm really not feeling well, Nurse

Green," I spoke, my voice seemed to catch in my throat and it came out roughly.

"I can tell," she said, wheeling back to the desk. "We found you dazed out in the hall. Let's see, which parent of yours would be easiest to get a hold of?"

She had pulled up the student directory on her tablet and was scrolling to the 'S' section.

"My Dad," I quickly stated.

He worked from home most days, so it would make the most sense for him to come and get me. Mom was all the way downtown and probably booked up with meetings all day.

Nurse Green tapped her screen, and the phone in her pocket started ringing. She fished it out and held it to her ear.

The ringing continued for a minute, and then abruptly ended. Nurse Green tapped another button on the tablet. Again, the phone started ringing and then promptly stopped.

She looked puzzled.

"What is it?" I asked. I had removed the compress; it was giving me a bit of brain freeze.

75

She returned the tablet and her phone back to the desk. She then picked up the receiver on an older, clunkier phone that sat next to her computer screen.

I sat up, her brow was furrowing deeper and deeper now.

"What?" I cried. "What's wrong?"

"At first, all I was getting was a busy signal. But now, I can't seem to even *get* a signal."

CHAPTER 15

Nurse Green asked if I was feeling hungry, and if she should bring back some lunch for me. I politely declined.

She returned twenty minutes later.

"You really dodged a bullet there," the nurse proclaimed. "I couldn't even look at whatever they were dishing up."

She grabbed her purse and keys from the desk drawer.

"You'll be alright if I run next door and

grab a burger or something, right?"

I nodded.

I was asleep before she even returned.

I woke up again with a jolt.

I was back in class.

Everyone was laughing.

"Dude, I think—" Dean started.

"Yeah yeah, I drooled." I snapped back, zipping up my jacket once more.

I stood up before Mrs. Teagan spoke; this took her by surprise.

"Mr. Shiner, I was hoping we were going to finish out the year with at least *one* day you didn't fall asleep in this classroom," she said, the class ate it up as always.

"Yeah, I'm sorry about that. Not much I can do about it now." I replied.

She cocked her head to one side and looked at me.

"Right..." she said, plucking up the same black expo marker I knew I wasn't going to be able to use. The very same one Lauren would solve the problem I couldn't in just a few short moments.

"Since you're up," she continued, "I

would like you to showcase to the class how we can solve this equation."

I was walking towards the front now. I could see out of the corner of my eye Lauren was turned to look at me.

What I would have given not to look like a complete chump in this moment.

My eyes hovered over the equation.

It was still the *same* as it had always been.

I had seen Lauren solve this a handful of times already, so...

That was it.

I already knew the answer!

Putting a little more hitch into my step, I snatched the marker from Mrs. Teagan with a fun flourish, who stepped backward, her eyes wide. I began to work.

Well, work was a very *loose* way of putting it, since I was just copying the answer.

It's not like this was cheating or anything...

Right?

I solved for X, Y, and that tricky Q.

I held the marker back to Mrs. Teagan, and turned to head back to my seat, feeling rightfully smug.

Now I knew how Vic felt most days. He had always been pretty smart.

"Very good, Mr. Shiner..." came from Mrs. Teagan.

I gave a wink to Dean, and took my seat.

"Except..." She was continuing. Mrs. Teagan was looking intently at the board. She pointed to where I had written the sum for Y. I had put down 28. "Y is thirty-eight, I'm afraid."

Dean grimaced and turned away from me, hiding his laughter.

Was it *always* thirty-eight?

I guess I didn't pay attention as well as I had hoped.

I slumped down low into my seat.

The clock read 9:58 a.m.

I would show them tomorrow, there was no way I was going to forget those answers.

CHAPTER 16

I threw my math book into my locker. I ended up throwing my whole bag in with it, too.

Dean opened up his own next to me, and jumped when I slammed mine shut.

"Hey, keep your phone hidden," I whispered, looking nervously over my shoulder.

He stared back, and gave me an odd look. I'm sure I looked crazy.

"Okay... " he replied, placing his math book away. "Oh wait, there is a video I have to show you real quick!"

He moved to unzip the phone from his backpack, but I grabbed his arm.

"Cat. Bag. Circles. Funny."

Dean stood frozen, his mouth opened in bewilderment.

"How—how did you know?" He stammered, his mouth was working like a fish out of water.

My eyes fell onto Coach G, who had just lumbered into the hallway. Even for his size, he moved swiftly and with agile grace. What you would expect from a lifetime athlete.

His head did a quick scan and paused on the two of us.

I let go of Dean, but he still stood transfixed.

In an instant, Coach G had covered the span of the hallway and stood in front of us.

"Morning, Mr. Brown, Mr. Shiner..." He muttered through gritted teeth.

This snapped Dean momentarily out of his trance.

"Oh, morning Coach!" He shot out, turning to close his locker and keep his phone hidden.

"Yeah, morning," I replied sarcastically.

Dean and Coach snapped their heads to look at me.

"I'll tell you this boys," Coach began, volleying his attention between the two of us. "You don't last very long in my profession if you don't have a good *nose* for when someone is up to no good. Let's not make any trouble. After all, it's our last day together," he growled.

His head turned to me and that's when I noticed something other than my warped reflection in his sunglasses.

Sniff, sniff.

When Coach had mentioned his nose, if he knew it or not, his own had begun flaring. Opening and closing rapidly, it was working overtime.

My cold sweat broke out over my back and neck.

Could Coach be what was in the bathroom a few days ago? No, that was *today.* I had to start getting that right if I was going to keep repeating. Technically it *was* a few days ago to me.

He stretched out his beefy arms and grabbed both of us by the shoulders, giving a firm squeeze. Maybe firm by his measurement, but to us it felt like he was trying to break our bones.

And then he was gone, resuming his patrol.

I was just glad I didn't have to do any more pushups.

"Thanks man, I owe you one," Dean smiled, throwing a hand up for a high five.

I met his hand instinctively, the movement in my shoulder shot a small amount of pain through it.

But my head was elsewhere.

There was only one thing I could do if I was going to get to the bottom of who that was outside Ms. Blithe's art room.

As much as I hated the idea, I was going to have to lie in wait for their return after lunch...

CHAPTER 17

Dean and I hurried to history class, but another thought occurred to me. One of my *worst* thoughts, actually.

"Hey, can we talk for a sec?" I asked my best friend, pulling him to the side of the door.

"Yeah, is it about what's up today? You seem... off..." he commented, looking me up and down.

I took a deep breath.

"I don't know how to explain it, Dean,

but..." I paused again, trying to guess how best to explain this situation to my friend.

Surely he would get it–we had a way of understanding each other better than most.

I stole one more quick glance around the now deserted hall.

"My day has been... repeating." I finally said.

Dean looked blankly at me.

Was he not going to believe me?

I tried to course-correct.

"Like, you know that old movie about the weatherman who keeps living the same day over and over?"

Dean slowly nodded, and his eyes narrowed.

"Yeah! So that's what's happening to me, today! That's how I knew about the phone, how we also have a test coming up," I pointed to the classroom behind him. "Even the math problem on the board. Do you think I could figure that out on my own and even get *one* answer correct? I don't know what to do here, man."

Dean was silent for longer than was comfortable. He then blinked a few times. I should have expected what was coming next.

"That is... such a *lame* joke, *bro*."

He really extended the 'O' on *bro*.

My heart dropped.

Dean's face broke out into a wide smile, in fact it almost looked sinister, and he couldn't help but laugh when he next spoke.

"You're *really* weirding me out today. Also, hello, this is *Mr. Meyer*. What do you mean a test? I don't think we even had one all year! Vic was right..."

Dean broke away and disappeared inside the classroom.

Right? Right about what?

I stood there in the empty hall feeling stupid.

"Oh, Freddy!" A voice called out.

I turned to see Mr. Meyer with a tall stack of paper rushing down the hall.

"Would you mind getting the door for me? I was tied up talking with the gym teacher, I almost didn't get these done!" He spoke, his words shooting off like rapid fire.

I grabbed the door handle and swung it

open. Mr. Meyer ducked inside and I was about to follow, but I heard Dean's voice clearly. He was slung onto his desk and had Aaron and Vic close by.

"...tries to tell me his day is on repeat!" Dean cackled. The other two threw back their heads and the three laughed together.

I quietly shut the door and ran all the way to the bathroom without looking back.

CHAPTER 18

I pulled my legs up and curled into myself in the last stall. I tried to breathe normally, but it was hard and my body shuddered like I was cold.

How could Dean talk about me like that?

How *long* had he been talking about me behind my back?

These questions and more danced around in my head. When I had felt I had gotten over one of them, another would barge in and bring me right back down, starting the whole process over again.

My mind flashed to what would happen when I was finally found in here, skipping class.

Who cares if they do? It'll just start over again. Duh, Freddy.

My day was on repeat. I just had to wait it out and everything would go back to how it was.

Even Dean would reset.

That made me feel better, but I wondered how I was going to react.

My mind didn't reset.

The floodgate had been opened. No easy way of fixing *that*.

I sat in that stall all through history, gym, and even past lunch. Several waves of students came in, and then the worst case scenario played out before I had even considered it.

Dean, Aaron, and Vic stopped by right after lunch.

My eyes grew wide when I recognized the approaching voices from the hallway.

They were laughing about something I

couldn't overhear. Couldn't still be me, right?

One of them closed the door to the stall next to mine and seemed to be spitting and dry heaving over the toilet.

That must have been Vic. Of course, the cafeteria food got him again.

"You do have to admit, it's kinda weird we had a test," Aaron commented.

His voice was out by the sinks, near the exit. Dean's was pretty close, too, I could tell when he spoke next.

"I know! Mr. Meyer, what happened?" Dean replied.

Aaron snorted. "He's probably on the chopping block. My parents weren't too impressed at conference night."

"Not really *our* problem now," Dean cheesed.

Vic next to me flushed.

He unlatched the stall door, and the three left without washing their hands.

Gross.

Even though the seat hurt to sit on for prolonged amounts of time (by design, I bet) I stayed in the bathroom the rest of the day.

My butt was sore and felt like it had taken on the shape of the toilet seat, but the moment of truth was coming up. No matter *what* I was still feeling, answers felt like a good bandage to... *something*.

I didn't know what yet.

From inside the bathroom I could see a clock hanging in the hallway. It had one of those big bells above it that rang at the end of the day. The lunch room had one, too. Together, those two were enough to make noise each day for the whole school.

The minute hand crept towards the top of the hour. Last time I had taken the pass at the start of class, after lunch. I needed to get into position!

I poked my head around the corner of the bathroom entrance and immediately pulled it back in.

My whole class was standing *right there!*

I'm so stupid, of course they were. We were supposed to be in art class, but Mrs. Teagan would bring us back to her room instead!

In fact, I heard her voice as soon as I thought that, and in no time, she was leading the students away. It was a good thing they were all facing the other way to begin with.

My eyes darted to the clock counting down the minutes. Any moment now, the time I had originally taken the pass to the bathroom would happen and I was going to see who was in the hallway finally.

The clock kept on. It was time.

I looked up and down the hall.

Nothing.

Then it was gone.

Many more minutes went by.

Before I knew it, the lunch room doors opened up and third graders burst into the hall. I ran back to the stall and threw the door shut behind me with no time to spare.

I heard voices again, many of them, coming from the hallways towards the bathroom.

A few came into the bathroom, laughing and making fart noises.

I expected the same kid to mention the hall pass, when I realized I *never* took it this time. It was still hanging up in Mrs. Teagan's room.

My stall door jiggled as another boy tried to open it up. I held my breath and stayed quiet.

Another teacher called into the bathroom and told them to hurry up. After a few minutes, they were all gone. Once again, I felt like the only living soul in the bathroom and hallway.

I exited the bathroom yet again.

Whoever that person with the creepy voice was didn't show up again.

What could that mean?

I had changed Mr. Meyer being late to class by giving Coach the slip earlier in the hallway. Could that have maybe changed this from happening too?

I had hoped so badly to catch this person. I made a vow I was going to try repeating the exact events of that day again, to catch this person—even if it meant I was going to have to do pushups again.

Who could it be? The answer was driving me nuts. They were looking for *someone*, but weren't looking for them here, like they did before?

A sudden terrifying thought occurred to me.

Could whatever that was happening to *me*,

be happening to *them* as well?

I dipped back into the bathroom again. I suddenly felt exposed and needed more privacy. This was the only place I could get it.

The remaining hours of the day went by slowly.

Every noise I heard, I recoiled with fear. I made up my mind I wanted *nothing* to do with whoever this was.

Finally, the bell rang out again.

It was so loud, *too loud*. It made my head spin.

─────CHAPTER 19─────

"Dude, I think you were drooling," Dean whispered to me.

I was back in class again, the disorientation of waking up wasn't as bad when I had spent a few hours ready for it.

I clenched my jaw, ignoring Dean altogether.

Let them see the spit line running down my shirt.

It's not like they would ever remember.

"Mr. Shiner, I was hoping we were going to finish out the year with at least *one* day..." she paused as I had already risen to my feet and met her at the board before she had finished. "...didn't fall asleep..." Mrs. Teagan softly spoke.

I grabbed a different color marker this time.

She stood back, slightly shocked that I was maybe *reading her mind*.

I wrote down (from memory) the correct answers. I clicked the marker back into place on the board and swiftly retreated back to my seat. I kept my head down the entire time. I didn't even look up when Mrs. Teagan clapped and cheered at the right answer.

"You *did* learn something this year, Mr. Shiner!" She cried out.

I grabbed tightly onto my math book and hurried away as Dean called out to me.

"Freddy, ayo?"

I passed by Coach G who was coming down the hall to where our lockers were. I remembered Dean and his phone. I would have to watch him get busted one of these days.

The hallway clock chimed, and soon after, the hallway cleared.

It was just me, strolling down the first grade wing.

The lights for half the hall were out, so it looked kind of creepy with it being all dark. I didn't know where I was headed exactly. Maybe I wanted to see what the other classes were doing.

The hairs on the back of my neck stood up, and I had this sudden urge to turn around.

I *wished* I hadn't.

At the end of the hall was a person.

It was hard to see anything other than their outline. What was even worse, they stood there, staring me down.

I couldn't see it, but I could *feel* it.

That's when I heard it again.

Sniff. Sniff. Sniff.

I was trapped. Behind me only exited to the gym or our cafeteria. But *then* where would I go?

The figure lowered their head and then charged at me.

It screamed in a blood curdling, high pitch

that sounded feral.

I turned to run. Where was I going? I didn't know, but I did not want this thing to catch me!

I rounded the corner to the last hall that led to the gym. I had to make a decision fast. Coach or lunch ladies? Which one would protect me?

That's when I saw something red on the wall.

It was a fire alarm. The big, white handle was down low for the smaller kids to reach.

I had heard a rumor when I was younger that there was a type of ink that sprayed out to mark the hands of any would-be-prankster. I didn't even think about that when I reached for it.

I heard the deranged person nearing me now, their scream was deafening.

Pulling hard, I yanked down the white handle and jumped back when my hand was suddenly wet. I held it up and saw it was black, just like the kids had said.

Then, the alarms in the ceiling started wailing. It cut off the scream of my chaser, perhaps startling them too.

Kids and teachers began pouring out of the classrooms in the hall. The head lunch lady opened the door to the cafeteria and looked down the hall, before shouting to the others to drop what they were doing and to follow.

They all exited and pointed at me. Together, the mass of them made a wall and began pushing me towards the hall I had just come down.

They rounded the corner and I saw that whatever had chased me was gone. My plan worked.

What didn't work, however, was the front doors everyone was exiting through.

They must not have noticed or even seen it the way I could, but they poured out through the doors, teachers and kids falling as soon as they cleared it.

It was like watching cattle be driven off a cliff, and I was being ushered towards my doom, too.

There was nothing I could do. I tried to pull away, but I felt a strong arm on the back of my neck.

I looked up and saw Coach G.

He looked really angry. That's when he grabbed my blackened hand and his mouth twisted into even greater fury.

He careened me to the nearest open doorway.

Then, he threw me through it, head first!

—— CHAPTER 20 ——

I pitched my math book into the first trashcan
I saw. Instead of going to my locker, I was going to hang back and watch Dean get busted.

I had spent the last ten minutes of class
calming down from having been throw into
the abyss. As expected, my day repeated
again.

With no one there to help Dean, Coach was
going to rip him, and only him, a new one.

And I had a front row seat.

Any moment now, Coach G would round the corner opposite of me, and the fun would begin. I couldn't help but smile.

Imagine my surprise when a meaty finger poked me in the back.

I jumped, and turned around to face *Coach G!*

He hadn't come from the hall he had been the other days, he was standing right behind me.

In his hands, was my math book. I knew it was mine, it had my name on it.

"Drop something, Freddy?" He growled.

Instead of making me do push-ups right there, Coach had me follow him to his office in the gym.

I trailed behind him, I couldn't believe my luck.

No pushups? I could handle that.

I didn't see him stop abruptly, and I ended up running right into him.

He was standing in front of our school's trophy case, staring proudly at it.

"Have you ever looked at these awards— and I mean really *looked* at them, Freddy?"

He asked, slowly turning to me.

"I've seen them before, but no, I guess I haven't?" I replied.

Coach turned back to the case.

"Each one of these awards were won by students who attended *this* school. From academics, to sports and... even one for an eating competition," he continued.

I looked into the case at some of the names.

Travis Beem: 200 Meter Dash. 1st place.

Amanda Fuller: State Science Fair Nominee.

Gerold Dunn: Pie Eating Contest Winner. Grade 4.

There was a photo accompanying this plaque of a kid smiling his dirty face from ear to ear.

The next one I noticed made me do a double-take.

Tabitha Blithe: Fine Arts.

There wasn't a photo, but *Blithe* and *arts*? It *had* to be my teacher Ms. Blithe, right? I thought so.

What I wouldn't give to talk with her at least one of these loops. She would be a great help, and I wouldn't have to worry too much about souring my image with her, since the day, and *she*, would both reset in the end.

I don't think in my entire time knowing her she ever had a bad thing to say about anyone else.

But she was nowhere to be found today.

The more names I read, the more I already understood where Coach was going to take his hallway lecture.

"I only see potential in my students. Potential that can easily contribute to this case."

He removed his sunglasses and slid them into his shirt pocket. For a large and very intimidating guy, his eyes were softer than I thought. I tried to think of a time he ever was seen without his glasses.

I couldn't.

Coach reached out a hand to put on my shoulder.

"Don't waste your potential, Freddy. *You* could be in that case."

I looked back into it. What could I excel at? I was pretty normal all around. They don't give awards for kids who have seen every

Camp Blood movie, and could quote them if provoked.

Coach continued.

"These years, being in school, can completely change your life if you let it. Don't waste your time here."

I wanted to laugh. *Waste time?*

I had nothing *but* time to waste.

He then continued to the gym, taking me through the dark hallway of the first graders, and forced me to run laps until next period started.

I was drenched to the bone by the time my class showed up. Coach split us into groups to inventory and pack up his equipment room again.

It was the one time I wished people didn't group Dean and I together for everything.

"Where were you last period?" Dean asked.

I ignored him and kept counting my stack of orange cones. He must not have noticed I was trying to ice him out.

"We had this quiz! *Mr. Meyer*, a quiz! Can you believe that?" He exclaimed, throwing his hands up.

I forced a smile. "Oh dang, that sucks."

"Yeah man, I only got half of them right!" He kicked over a stack of cones he had just counted. Several went skittering away. "Like, who knows when the Vietnam War ended?"

"1975," I said without thinking.

That was the answer to number two on the quiz.

Dean stared at me like I suddenly grew another head out of my shoulder.

I tried to quickly deflect. "I mean, everyone knows that, right?" In fact, I remembered most of the answers and could probably best even Vic now. *That* could be fun.

"Apparently not, that's one not even *Vic* got right!" Dean shouted.

Huh. I could score a perfect score. Vic always got one wrong. That would be fun to rub in his face.

My brain clicked.

That was my potential.

I had the ability to repeat the day over and over again! Sure I wouldn't be getting an award for acing Mr. Meyer's first and probably *last* test at Briarwood Elementary; but if I could clear the whole day with a perfect score...

That might be how I could escape!

I was too transfixed to notice Dean look up, his face turning white. He then ran.

I was so immediately caught up in this plan of mine that I never noticed the gym scoreboard falling down.

And I was standing right underneath it.

—— CHAPTER 21 ——

My eyes widened in fear. My legs seemed to feel a hundred pounds heavier. *There was no way I could move!*

I heard several classmates scream. My own would have been included, but no sound came out.

I was done for.

Would I still reset if I was flattened?

I *would* have found out, if it hadn't been for someone crashing into me. They wrapped their arms around me and together we flew out of the way.

A deafening *CRASH* shook the floor so bad, it left a giant dent from one side of the gym to the other.

"IS EVERYONE OKAY?!" I could hear Coach shouting over the cries from everyone else.

I was okay. I had been saved.

I had landed on my face.

I looked up and saw my best friend Dean standing there. He had run *away* from where we were standing just moments ago. I could have swore he would have moved to help me. There was a lot I was finding out about Dean every day. Or *repeats* of the same day.

A girl coughed down towards my middle section, and I turned to look who still had me wrapped up in their arms.

My heart skipped a beat.

It was Lauren.

She had scraped her arm, and it looked bad. She coughed again, and we found each other's eyes.

She gave me a smile.

I smiled back.

Lauren must have realized she was still attached to me, and she quickly moved to let go. We both stood up, but a pain in my side made me sit right back down.

It was hard to breathe suddenly. My side felt very hot.

Coach G was upon us. I tried standing again, but he insisted I stay put.

I clutched at my side.

Why did it hurt so bad?

"Don't move, Freddy. You may have cracked a rib," Coach said, his entire demeanor felt strangely nice. "Nice moves out there, Miss Palmer."

A few other students were clapping her on the back. She didn't seem to notice. Her arm was red and turning purple in places too, but she was still focused on *me*.

"Freddy, I'm sorry..." She started saying.

"Nonsense," Coach cried out. "We would have had one *flat Freddy* without you."

There's a nickname I was glad would *never* stick, thanks to the loops. That made me feel good.

I suddenly thought back to the hallway on my second loop. *I could have saved her.* I was *trying* to, at least. My mind still couldn't get past the fact that she had been the one to save *me* this time.

Had my thoughts been more focused, the immediate red flag would have been obvious.

The scoreboard never fell the other days.

It fell when *I* was under it.

I wouldn't know it until tomorrow's repeat when something much more horrible happened—but someone was after *me*.

───── CHAPTER 22 ─────

I spent the rest of the day in Nurse Green's office. She kept apologizing for the lack of service to call an ambulance. I figured as much would happen.

She once again asked if I was interested in lunch. I declined. For someone having not eaten for nearly a week now, I was doing pretty good!

When Nurse Green was returning, I overheard a voice speaking with her from the hallway.

"He's going to be okay, right?" The first voice said.

The second, which was clearly Nurse Green's, laughed and responded, "Of course, darling, it's a bruised or possibly cracked rib. Nothing serious!" She gave her trademark laugh a whirl at that.

Nothing serious to *her* maybe–my side hurt!

I crept up and off the bed to spy through the door window, ignoring the pain in my side.

I was once again shocked. It was Lauren.

She was really something else; first saving me and now checking up on me? It would be my lucky day if the day in question would stop repeating, and just let me enjoy the spoils of the days afterward.

I hobbled back into bed just in time as Nurse Green returned.

"You really dodged a bullet there," she proclaimed. "I couldn't even look at whatever they were dishing up."

I was glad I didn't have to today.

Maybe one of these days I would actually *try* it.

CHAPTER 23

I am *so glad* I didn't decide to try it on my next repeat day. My side still stung all throughout the rest of math and into history. It didn't look bruised, but it still felt tender. I couldn't explain it.

Mrs. Teagan was once again over the moon at my correct answers. Coach G gave Dean and me a firm warning after I had stashed his phone again. Mr. Meyer had to physically come to my desk to see the miracle that happened on my paper.

In big bold red ink: *10/10*.

I even put my name on it.

Vic looked mortified and didn't speak the rest of the class.

Instead of spreading the cones out to the middle of the gym, I kept us off to the side, looking up into the ceiling with nervous glances.

Dean noticed this a few times, and it made him quiet.

I glanced across the gym and could have sworn Lauren was looking at *me* first. She quickly moved and smoothly ducked behind someone else.

It was lunch time, and Vic was still upset about the test results. He poked around with his food, not touching a bite.

Dean jumped into the seat next to me and pulled a sandwich from his lunchbox. At the sight of the mountains of meatloaf, he coughed.

"What *is* that?" Dean turned his nose up at it.

"Apparently, it's meatloaf," Aaron had already said before, repeating it now for Dean.

"Yeah, I wouldn't eat that..." He muttered.

Vic looked distraught. I felt bad for making such a big deal about the test. Then I remembered what Dean had said about Vic.

"Vic was right..."

Something inside of me still felt guilty, even though I had every right not to be.

I turned to Vic. "Give it a shot, I bet it's better than it looks!"

Vic looked sideways at me. He picked up his fork and begrudgingly snatched up a bite.

His mood changed immediately.

He started shoveling more into his mouth.

"You can't seriously be eating that, Vic." Dean laughed.

I did too.

Aaron joined in as Vic went ham on his lunch. Someone from behind bumped into me. I didn't bother to turn around. It felt good to laugh with my friends again.

In a matter of seconds, Vic had completely devoured his tray. His eyes fell on Aaron's, and my own tray.

We both slid it over.

Vic pushed his tray away and pulled mine up.

"This ketchup is really good, too!" Vic blurted out.

It was still so watered down, it hardly resembled ketchup anymore. In fact, looking at it again, the one on my tray looked *darker*, more like *blood*, even.

"Man, I need to see if I can get the recipe to this—" Vic started saying as he stood up.

I waited for the inevitable throw up, but Vic trotted over to the one lunch lady scooping up limited trays.

Word must have gotten out, there was hardly a line.

She stuck her metal scooper into the mountain of oozing meat, and wrote something down on a piece of paper. She handed it to Vic, who quickly stored it in his back pocket.

The lunch lady smiled after him—that must have made her day.

He came back to our table.

"Man, you're crazy," Dean said, finishing his sandwich.

Vic rolled his eyes and scooped up a big

bite from my tray. He ate bite after bite after...

That's when his body started shaking.

A little late, but better than never.

Vic flew up and ran to the dumpster, but this time he didn't make it. Meat gurgled back up from his mouth, and he fell to his knees, retching harder and harder.

This seemed *worse* than the other times.

He just kept going.

His face was turning paler and paler. The growing chucks in front of him were incredible when you realized it all came from *one* kid!

That's when Vic make a choking sound.

The whole lunch room became deadly quiet, watching with baited breath.

Vic grasped at his throat, clawing at it, and fell forward into his own mess.

The meatloaf *was* dangerous!

This time it had *killed* Vic!

CHAPTER 24

Maybe I got ahead of myself. Vic didn't die, but he got as close as anyone could.

Aaron, Dean and I were pulled into the principal's office. He mentioned something about tampered food, and we all started talking at once.

It became very clear the food in question had come from my tray.

Dean and Aaron wasted no time by throwing me under the bus and claimed I had been acting weird all day. It was settled; until further investigations were made, I was to stay in the principal's office for the remainder of the day.

Principal Ong tried a few times to get an outside line, but never seemed to have any luck. I could have told him that, but I didn't know whether I should wait the day out, or run.

I ended up doing the latter.

A call came through his phone finally. It had a flashing light on it, indicating it was coming from somewhere else in the building.

Principal Ong lifted the headset and listened.

"I understand," he spoke, pausing for the other party to finish talking. They were talking fast from what I could hear, but I couldn't make out the voice.

He tried to interrupt a few times, but the other person on the line kept on. Every now and then, Ong raised his eyes to look at me.

"The fact of the matter is, this is out of my hands now," Ong had found a break in the conversation and took hold of it. "Nurse

Green has indicated several signs of..."

Principal Ong looked at me again before cupping his hand over the bottom of the phone. I still heard what he said.

"...*poison*. Until further help is available, we cannot let him back to his classes. You may talk with him, if I am present, and we will not be allowing Mr. Shiner to roam freely the rest of the day, am I understood?"

The voice on the other line was quiet for a few seconds until the dial tone indicated they had hung up.

Ong hung the phone back up and glared at me once more.

"Who was that?" I questioned.

"None of your business," was his only response.

Principal Ong would leave his office periodically, at which time the two secretaries would swivel in their chairs to keep watch of me.

After the fifth time of this, Ong left for awhile. Watching from my peripheral vision, the two secretaries didn't even turn around this time. I studied the clock in the office and it made sense—he was headed to his end of the year speech. I had made up my mind awhile ago, and I cautiously slipped out.

I didn't have to crawl, or do any quick rolls to avoid detection like I was envisioning. I simply just got up and walked out through the back office hallway.

Easy as that.

I wouldn't try it, though, if you ever find yourself in a similar situation.

Out of the office, I knew I couldn't afford to stay in the open; I had to find hiding quick.

Did I make my way back to the bathroom?

You bet I did.

Principal Ong's hushed word played in my head on repeat as if it was stuck in its own personal time loop of five seconds.

Posion.

Someone had poisoned Vic.

Well, tried to poison *me!*

I passed the trophy case again. There was an odd sense of failure that hit—that I wouldn't be part of these accomplishments. Part of these successful kids, some of which stayed here to help the next generation. In that moment, I wanted a do-over on my year. A moment to add to the collection.

I caught that thought and quickly tried to suppress it. One day was enough, I couldn't repeat the *entire year.*

I swiftly continued down towards the boy's bathroom when something else caught my eye.

I couldn't hide in the bathroom, they would find me now that they would be looking for me.

I hadn't even thought of hiding elsewhere until I saw the light on in the room. For the week of loops I had experienced, it was always dark—but now it wasn't.

It was Ms. Blithe's art room.

Someone was inside who *hadn't* been the other days.

CHAPTER 25

I couldn't tell you why I was reaching out to open the door to the art room. All the red flags were there. For all I knew that *person* from earlier in the hallway was the one in there!

There was really only one way to find out. I reached out to see if it was even unlocked.

It was.

I opened the door.

The room's lights were on. The fluorescent white glow was filtered through many colorful film layers embedded in the ceiling, casting the room in different colored spots.

I cautiously and slowly looked around. There didn't appear to be any signs of anyone other than me being in the room.

A loud *hiss* made me jump.

It was the hydraulic contraption on the door as it shut.

I wasn't the only one it made jump.

From under the desk in the back corner I heard a loud *THUMP!*

Fear engulfed me, and I felt clammy and hot all of a sudden. There was something *under* Ms. Blithe's desk!

I stood there, not sure what to do next. I was creeping closer to the source of the noise. My feet had a plan they didn't share with the rest of me.

Why am I doing this?

I was halfway across the room when I saw her face peeking from behind the side of the desk.

I didn't recognize her at first.

It was Ms. Blithe!

Her eyes looked wild, unlike herself.

When we saw each other, she looked more scared of me than I was of her. She quickly disappeared back into hiding under the desk.

"Ms. Blithe?" I called out.

Silence.

I took another step towards the desk. This time she emerged, standing fully up. She had something in her hands. It looked like a small bottle of perfume.

"Stay right where you are, or I'll make you wish you had," she commanded. Her eyes were wide with panic.

It took me longer than I care to say to figure out the bottle in her hand... was pepper spray.

It even had a picture of a bear on it.

That had to be the good stuff.

It made me stand up straighter—now *I* was the one beginning to panic. That's when I noticed how disheveled she looked. Her eyes were dark underneath, and her hair seemed to be standing on end in some places. This was not the normal Ms. Blithe I knew.

"What are you doing in here, Freddy?" She demanded, shaking the mace at me.

"I–I saw the lights on, and... and..." I began, not sure where I was headed, or how I could explain myself.

"You're supposed to be in Mrs. Teagan's class right now, *pretending* to read a book."

Her eyes softened slightly. She was starting to calm down. The initial shock had startled her, but it was just me, *Freddy*, her favorite fifth grader!

"Well, I have been in the principal's office since lunch, and–wait..." I started but fell silent, my mind working overtime. "How did you know what I did the first day?"

Ms. Blithe lowered the mace. Her eyes looked wet, like she was about to cry.

"So it *is* you," she muttered. Her mind seemed to be working overtime, too.

"What do you mean, Ms. Blithe?" I was completely lost.

"Freddy..." She rounded the corner of the desk. "This happened to me when I was your age, too. And it's happening to me again now."

129

CHAPTER 26

"You what? What's happening?" I spoke a million miles per hour. "You know? Where have you been? How did it stop? *How do I stop it?!*"

The energy seemed to sap out of Ms. Blithe. She slumped backwards and sat on her desk.

"I don't know, Freddy..." She sighed.

"That's just great!" I yelled, throwing my hands up and turning away. I was going to be stuck looping this day forever.

"You seem to at least be in well enough spirits," Ms. Blithe commented. She was really looking rough, like she hadn't slept in days. Weeks, maybe.

Every time I looked at her, she averted her eyes. It was surreal seeing her this way.

She then continued, "After a hundred or so times around, I would feel...well..." she then gestured to herself.

I faced her again; something about what she said made me think.

"Did you say a *hundred times?*"

She nodded, as if I had just asked if the sky was blue.

"Yes, aren't you getting bored and tired yet?" She looked at me. She seemed to brighten up each minute we talked.

"I've, what do I call it, *looped*, only about ten times or so. Maybe not even that many..." I trailed off, trying to count.

Ms. Blithe jumped up and reached out towards me, grabbing both of my arms tightly.

"Ten times, *ten times*, TEN TIMES?!" She was yelling now. I had never seen her so much as raiser her voice before. "You aren't lying to me, Freddy?"

"N–no, honestly, Ms. Blithe!" I replied, I must have looked scared, because she stopped herself and instead gave me a hug.

She was very warm, and honestly after what I had been going through, it felt really nice.

"I'm sorry... I don't have the faintest idea what is going on. But you say you've only looped maybe *ten* times?"

She held me out at arms length. I nodded.

"I was wondering why you and everyone else seemed to be normal each day."

"How many times have you repeated this day, Ms. Blithe?" I questioned. She swallowed hard. I was suddenly scared of the answer.

"I lost count after I followed each student in the building a few days in a row."

I did the math.

Loosely, of course.

There were about eighty fifth graders alone, not to mention the entire school. The number was closer to six-hundred. We did have quite a large school.

If she had followed everyone for multiple days...

She had been looping today well over a few *thousand times*.

CHAPTER 27

"How did you escape from this last time, Ms. Blithe?" I asked.

We had locked the door for safety with one of those cords. We sat in the middle of the room facing each other.

Ms. Blithe licked her lips a few times before speaking.

"I was your age, actually," She spoke softly. "It was the first day of school for me," Ms. Blithe shuddered. I think I did, too. Repeating the first day for me would have been worse.

"Here I was repeating the same day over and over. I was so nervous the entire summer about fifth grade. I spent most of my days studying, while others were outside playing, or going to camp."

I nodded. I wondered if I would ever have the chance to do the same.

"You can see how frustrating that would be, to spend all your time preparing for something that would *never* happen."

"Yeah, the first day is never a *real* day, no matter what school you're in." I agreed.

"Right. I wanted to become a doctor, or work for NASA, or–I don't know, something only a smart person could do. My older sister did alright for herself, and the pressure was on for me to do the same. But I just couldn't move forward. I read all my text books, rifled through file cabinets for future tests–anything to feel like I was making a difference!"

She yelled the last part. This must have been what PTSD was like. I wondered if I would feel the same if I ever got back to a normal life.

Ms. Blithe fixed herself before continuing. A small amount of the teacher I knew was there, if only for a moment while she was embarrassed.

"I started doing *anything* I could, anything I could *learn*, and that's—that's when I fell in love."

Her eyes were sparkling, again; a little more of the teacher I had know for years was coming back.

"Was it someone in your class?" I asked. I was beginning to get invested now. It was hard to see adults as people who were once just like me.

She scowled at the question and shook her head.

"No, no, no, no—not *that* kind of love. I found what I was *passionate* about. *Art!*"

I looked around the room. The walls were covered with works done by Ms. Blithe. Many were very good. Sketches, to oil paintings, and even smaller sculptures that weighed a ton near the back.

The first time I had stepped into her room, I felt energized. I wanted to make drawings like hers. I struggled with it at first, but she had given me many useful tips that took my doodles from *crude*—to *dynamic*.

"Art is not something one can just *do*. Well, unless you're truly talented... But something you must *build*. I had many, many days devoted to making new and exciting pieces. There was only one problem..."

I guessed it before she said it. "You never got to finish them."

She nodded and ran her fingers through her hair. That helped her appearance a little.

"I would have spent more time working on it, but every day would reset, sometimes right before I was done. I had to get better. I pushed myself day after day to get *faster*, but that's when..." She paused.

For the first time since this strange day had started, she looked at me, *really* looked at me, and I could tell she was holding something back.

"... I ended the loop." She finished.

Her story strengthened my theory.

She was put in a loop to expand her horizons towards something more for her, more personal. Maybe that's what *I* had to do too?

"I have an idea, Ms. Blithe."

She sat back in her chair.

I continued, "I think something has to be said for your loop being the first day, and mine being the last day."

Her lips curled into a small smile. "Go on."

"If your loop ended once you unlearned what was expected of you and followed your passion, what if–" I shook my head, I didn't want to be right, "what if mine is the opposite? I can't leave the school without knowing what's expected of me. Maybe if I can clear the day without a hiccup or missing questions on tests–"

She interjected, "I noticed that too, a test? I want to move forward a day if only to see what happens to Mr. Meyer's job."

She had a point. Dang, now I was curious, too.

"Well? Could it work?" I asked.

"It might. But there's an issue."

I cocked my head to the side.

Issue, what issue?

"Freddy, when I looped, I found out there

was another teacher who was also looping. He did—bad things."

That's when my encounter popped back into my head.

"Ms. Blithe, on one of my first days looping, someone I think was looking for you. They were right outside your door!"

Ms. Blithe got suddenly very quiet.

"I know. There's another person looping."

──CHAPTER 28──

"There's another?" I stammered.

Ms. Blithe nodded. "They've been hiding very well, but there should be no reason for them to stay hidden like this... unless..."

Ms. Blithe got up and peeled back some loose paper that was covering the window by the door. She then quickly turned off the lights to the room. It took a moment for my eyes to adjust. The windows only offered minimal light through the coverings taped to them.

That's when I heard footsteps running in the halls.

"Check the bathroom!" I heard Principal Ong command.

The door handle rattled, and then fell silent.

"Art room is clear, locked!" Came the voice of Mr. Meyer.

It was a search party, looking for me.

How lovely.

Ms. Blithe folded the window blocking paper back into place and paced back and forth by the door.

I broke the silence finally.

"Ms. Blithe—there have been things happening that haven't happened before."

She turned to stare at me.

"Like what? Different how?"

"Well, today for starters, in the lunch room, I think someone tried to poison me. And yesterday..." I trailed off.

"Someone tried to flatten you in the gym." Ms. Blithe finished.

"Yeah, that's exactly it! The scoreboard fell and would have crushed me!"

Ms. Blithe looked to the ground. Her head bobbed there for a split second. "This other teacher, I think is trying to figure out which one of the students is looping. Two days in a row, I think they figured out it's you."

Make that *three* with cornering me in the hall. I jumped up from my seat.

"But I need to finish the day with one hundred percent if we're going to move forward! How can I do that when someone is trying to actively take me out?" I realized how corny that sounded once it was out loud. What was I in, a video game?

She put a finger to her lips and closed her eyes, thinking hard. "I know you're looping now, you know I'm looping now. What if I helped you complete your day? That would make it go back, right? The loop would stop?"

"I–I don't know, *you're* the expert here! I have a strong feeling if I do, we can escape!" I said.

"Tomorrow, let's do our best to memorize everything. You're going to clear it, and I'm going to help keep an eye on you!"

I knew finding Ms. Blithe would help.

I just had to focus and make sure to end this as soon as possible.

Should be easy? *Right?*

CHAPTER 29

It wasn't.

We both waited out the day in the art room.

I was a nervous sketcher, so that's what I did.

Ms. Blithe sat by herself at the desk in the back and kept her eyes closed.

I dropped my pen when the bell in the hallway rang loudly. Ms. Blithe didn't even move.

I had already memorized the answers to

Mrs. Teagan's math problem, and without fail, she was showering the praise down on me.

I watched out for Dean, and kept his phone hidden between class. That's when *another* idea struck me.

I quickly pulled out a sheet from the bottom of my locker and wrote down the ten answers.

I shoved it into Dean's hands.

"Don't ask, but memorize these answers."

I looked around cautiously before waltzing into Mr. Meyer's class.

Dean still looked puzzled, but I could see his lips moving as he read the answers.

"Give it to Aaron next," I whispered.

Dean hesitantly looked at me, but still offered the sheet to Aaron. He looked just as confused.

Vic took his seat on the other side of Aaron.

It was good to see him walking around.

"Psst, hey Vic," I whispered to him next. "1975. Nine-teen-seventy-five." I held up my fingers as I mouthed the numbers.

He looked at me, joining the club of confused friends at the back of the room. He and Dean shared a look.

The test was handed out shortly after.

I did my best to ignore the stares from the three next to me. If my plan had gone right, we'd all be acing this test.

I passed my test forward to the girl sitting in front of me to grade. Taking hers, I uncapped my pen and stared down in horror.

The questions were all different.

I hadn't even noticed and just wrote down the answers I had remembered.

Somehow, the test had changed!

CHAPTER 30

"What was that all about, man?" Dean pestered me as we walked into the gym. I still nervously looked up at the black scoreboard.

"I - uhh, someone from the class before tipped me off about the test."

Dean knew I was lying. He turned and walked away to join the rest of the class. Lauren was standing near the group by Coach's office, and was staring at me, *again*.

If I had any nerve, I would just talk to her.

What's the worst I could do, make a fool of myself?

The day would reset. She would never know.

Unless I made a fool of myself and the day *didn't* reset.

That was a scarier prospect.

The door to the hall opened slightly, and Ms. Blithe stuck her face in.

"Freddy, come here!" She whispered.

A few of the students turned to look at her.

I jogged back the way I came and exited out into the hallway.

If I had been startled to see Ms. Blithe as disheveled as she was yesterday, you can imagine my surprise when she looked *mostly* normal now.

The bags under her eyes were still heavy, and she still looked very tired. She took me by the arm, and moved me away from the door to the gym.

"How's the day going? Anything different?" She asked.

My stomach sank.

"Yeah... the test was different. Different

questions. Different answers."

She closed her eyes. I could see the muscles in her face tensing.

"Was Mr. Meyer any different?" She spoke quickly.

I had to think about it. He still seemed his usual self. Other than the answers he read out loud, everything else had been the same.

"No. Same old, same old." I responded. "I did try to tip off my friends with the answers, do you think that could have anything to do with it?"

"Yes. Anything you do can also change the days. Stick to getting yourself through the day, and we'll worry about everyone else later! Get back to class, you have cones to count." She smiled, then turned to leave.

I went back inside the gym. Coach G was already out and in the middle of the court. Everyone else was spread out along the edge of the gym.

No one was doing inventory today.

Everyone was running.

Coach blew his whistle and pointed to the floor in front of him. I jogged over to him.

"Where do you think you were, Mr. Shiner?"

"Sorry, I was talking to a teacher."

"Who?" He barked and leaned in closer.

"Ms. B–Teagan. She was returning something I forgot in her class this morning..."

Coach blew his whistle again.

"Get moving, we're going to spend the hour running!"

My day went from easy mode to hard real quick.

CHAPTER 31

I passed on even grabbing a tray for lunch. This didn't stop Vic, who once again put away his own tray, and Aaron's, before having to make a quick stop.

I kept scanning the lunch room, but everything seemed normal again.

Even Vic over by the trash cans.

Ms. Blithe's room was still dark, so after lunch we all returned to Mrs. Teagan's class again.

"Can't believe the nerve of some people..." She muttered under her breath as we
took our seats.

Lauren raised her hand.

"Mrs. Teagan, why wasn't Ms. Blithe in
her classroom?" She asked.

Mrs. Teagan laughed out loud and shook
her head. "That's what we all would like to
know. Class, take out your final book study
sheets and make sure they're complete before the end of the hour."

Was I expected to clear this day by finishing *this*? There was no way I was going to be
able to read even *one* of the books before this
evil looper would get me.

I walked over to the bookshelf and grabbed
the most recent book we had finished in our
homeroom class.

The title was boring, and flipping it over,
the first paragraph on the back was somehow
even worse. But as I scanned on, I knew I had
read this before.

No, I had seen it before!

Of course! It was last year's big summer
blockbuster that didn't include a superhero.

Dad and I went to see it, and we talked about it for days after.

This was a book?

They always say books are better than the movies, but I never believed them because— who can finish a whole book in less than two hours?

Exactly.

I opened the book up and started reading. Maybe whatever was watching over Ms. Blithe and me would still give me points for trying.

From the first page, I could see the movie playing out in my head. There was more detail in the words, and more scenes that were missing or changed completely from the movie. They were much better in the book, and I wished I could watch the version of the movie that followed what I was reading more closely.

I was nearing the end of chapter seven when Mrs. Teagan clapped her hands. Does anyone get to the end of a chapter and *then* get interrupted? Not even the luckiest person in the world could swing that. I ripped a piece of scrap paper and put it into the book, not re-alizing I would have to re-find my place the next time around.

The whole class filed out, and I once again sat through the entire speech by Principal Ong. I tried to focus on what I had learned today.

I needed to do things by myself, otherwise everything would change.

I needed to keep an eye open at all times to make sure I wasn't an easy target for whoever was sabotaging my days.

But most importantly of all, I needed to try and talk with Lauren.

I knew my opportunity would be perfect at the end of the day as we all were cleaning out lockers. I didn't bother with mine.

I nervously approached her, everything I had thought of saying had disappeared. My mind was blank.

That's when she turned around.

"Oh, hello Freddy," she calmly said, push-ing her hair behind her ear.

"Uhh, hey," I said hesitantly.

We both stood there staring at each other.

"What's up?" She finally asked.

"Would you—want to sometime this summer—uhh—hang out?" I choked. My tongue felt three times larger.

Surprisingly, she smiled.

"You maybe said only a handful of things to me this year, but want to *hang out?*" She asked.

I looked down. I had been harboring my feelings for her all year, but never made any sort of move to even talk with her. This was like a *total stranger* coming up to you and asking to hang out over the summer.

"That sounds fun," she finished.

I couldn't help but gawk at her.

"Really? I mean, cool—cool, yeah. Maybe at the pool or something?" Was it really this easy?

"That sounds like fun!" She said.

We both stood there, looking around. I don't think either of us knew what to do next.

One of her friends waved her over from down the hall.

She smiled once more and said, "Alright, well..."

"Yeah, yeah," was my only response.

We smiled at each other once more, and then we split and went opposite ways.

My head was in the clouds!

How was talking to a girl, *that girl*, so easy? What had I been afraid of all this time? I felt sad this was about to reset again, but if things were that easy, there was no way I couldn't just repeat this conversation again after I escaped.

I practically skipped down the hallway, happy as can be. I heard the bell once more, and Dean was telling me about my shirt again.

I was back in the morning class.

We went through our normal script; I took the marker and wrote down the three answers. I capped it and handed it back to my teacher who was again in shock.

On my way back, Lauren and I locked eyes. This time I didn't feel the urge to quickly look away. Instead, I smiled. She flashed the same smile as a few minutes ago. It made my heart do a little flutter.

Today was going to be the one I finally ended this looping business. Start with the right answer in math, right answers for my-self in history, and maybe I could get a few more chapters cranked out of my book before the day was over again.

In fact, I knew the movie pretty well; I might be able to expedite the answers there, too. I made a quick detour over to the shelf and grabbed the same copy I had started yes-terday.

Once back in my seat, I leafed through the book. I couldn't remember if I was on chapter seven or eight, so I folded both corners of the chapters to be safe.

I normally would *never* do that, but the book would be fine, it would reset.

I started on the book, and that's when I no-ticed it was quiet in the room.

Too quiet.

I stared up at Mrs. Teagan.

She hadn't burst out into hysterics at the right answer like before. She was still staring at the board.

"Freddy–I..." She started, but trailed off.

That's when I looked at the board and real-ized today was not going to be the day.

The problem was different, so of course my answers didn't match. How could things have already changed *this* much?

———— CHAPTER 32————

"Did you change anything?" Ms. Blithe questioned me.

I was sitting in her darkened classroom again. I had skipped meeting Coach in the hall, and the test in history class.

"No, I had just restarted! I couldn't have done anything!" I cried.

Ms. Blithe rocked back in her chair. She closed her eyes and began running her fingers through her hair once more.

"This is troubling, Freddy," she said through her fingers, which were now pulling her face back.

Ms. Blithe let go, and her face returned to normal.

I sat there trying to figure out what was happening *and why.* Was this something to do with the third looper? *How could that be?*

I had an idea.

"What if..." I started, trying to pick the best words I could to get my teacher to follow. "What if it's *supposed* to be like this?"

She blankly stared at me. "What are you getting at?"

I started again.

"What if I'm not supposed to just memorize answers for the day? What if I'm actually supposed to get up in front of the class this morning, and actually *solve* a math problem?"

Ms. Blithe let out a long sigh.

"Freddy, you're not much for academics, I'm afraid. That could take as many days as we had in the school year."

That was a lot.

I didn't know if I was prepared to work that hard, for that long, without knowing for sure if it would work.

"You could help me," I started rambling. "We could meet here everyday, and work on different things!"

I pulled the paperback book from my bag.

"I can start with this. I've already made some progress, and if I don't have to worry about anything else, I can finish it in a whole loop!"

My art teacher's eyes fell to the floor.

"But you're not passionate about studying. That's how I got out of *my* loop. Art saved me."

She was right. I despised studying. Maybe that wasn't the way out, but neither was giving up, which it looked like she was doing.

"Ms. Blithe..."

She raised a finger and pointed to the door.

"Get out, Freddy. I need to think," she said in a low voice.

CHAPTER 33

I didn't see Ms. Blithe again for a few days.

Loops. Whatever.

I went ahead and tried my plan. Sure enough, each day now reset with different math problems, different test questions, and Coach made us run *each* period now.

The soreness I felt washed away each loop, but a small amount still remained and started building. Without realizing, it was getting easier and easier to keep running the full hour. Cutting through the stage was easier, too. I felt I could hop and bound over the items on muscle memory alone!

Just like it was easier to run, so was it to read. I put a considerable dent in the first book until I came up with a foolproof idea.

I grabbed the book first thing in the loop after I woke up from my nap, and took refuge in the bathroom to finish it. My legs hurt so bad after one loop in there I decided to find another space.

The library was mostly empty throughout the day. The aides gave me funny looks, but I brought my own books and wasn't messing up their progress of tidying up the shelves for summer.

One loop, I studied from my history textbook. I wasn't sure what was going to appear on the test until I looked a few sections ahead and saw familiar questions at the end of each chapter.

Mr. Meyer had pulled these right from the book himself!

I know I was on a mission to actually try and learn this stuff, and I was thankful in that moment. There ended up being hundreds, if not more, of these example questions.

On a different loop, I did the same with my math work. I was able to ask the same library aide on multiple days different questions, and she helped me each time happily at understanding some basic concepts.

I never skipped gym though. I was starting to actually like running.

Me! Who would have thought?

I also didn't just finish the one book for our report, I finished almost half the list! Not all of them were my favorites, like the first, but I started enjoying seeing new and different ways someone could write and tell a story.

I felt like I could maybe do that someday, too. The more I thought about it, the more it sounded right.

I was never quite able to get Vic to stop from throwing up in the cafeteria. I tried limiting his food, but he ended up going back for more. I asked Nurse Green for some sickness relief medicine, and tried coaxing him to take it, which he wouldn't.

Nothing worked.

I had to think up some new ways, but I ended up just skipping lunch altogether after a few times.

The only part of my day I really looked forward to was the end of the day when Lauren and I were able to talk by the lockers.

We discussed many topics, including her favorite bands (I made a mental note to look those up sometime), places her family had been to and she had seen, and even simple things, like actual school work. She was quick to explain a problem I was struggling with, even with the aide's help, and it always clicked with her.

She didn't know it, but she might just be able to save me once again.

The best part about all of this, I was either very lucky, or the third looper had decided not to try and kill me. It helped that I was moving around a lot during the loops. I also kept my eyes peeled for *anything* different.

I was on track, nearing the end of both text books in my loops, when on one loop, while in Mrs. Teagan's class in the afternoon, there was a knock at the door.

Moments later, Ms. Blithe stepped inside.

"Sorry to interrupt, but Freddy needs to come to the office with me," she said plainly.

I brightened up. I couldn't wait to tell her all about what I had learned and accomplished in these handfuls of loops. The door was locked every time I had tried to go into the art room. I knew that sometimes adults needed their space and I was more than okay giving it to her, even if it made me feel more lonely.

Mrs. Teagan was on her feet, arms crossed over her body.

"And why is it that your classes have been discontinued today? This is my free hour and–,"

"Flooding," Ms. Blithe interrupted. "The whole classroom has been shut down."

"Oh, oh dear, I am so sorry. Your works?"

"Gone, I'm afraid," The whole class was tuned in. Ms. Blithe could have easily become an actress with performances like this. She had Mrs. Teagan *completely* fooled!

Ms. Blithe cleared her throat.

"Freddy?" She called back to me. "You're

needed in the office."

I got up and left my stuff there. It would revert back in a few hours, anyway.

Out in the hallway, Ms. Blithe shut the door. She then turned to me.

"Freddy, I know how to get out of this loop! I've figured it out."

I almost yelled out loud. This was incredible! I knew I could count on Ms. Blithe!

I did momentarily feel dumb wasting so much time in my loops on studying, but I didn't care if I could still get out of this mess *and* earlier than I had hoped.

"That's amazing! What do we need to do?" I cried out.

Ms. Blithe smiled.

"Let's go back to the room, we can discuss it there."

She started down the hallway, and I skipped after her.

It wasn't even the summer break I was missing most. My family, my room and bed, even eating anything other than what was being served in the lunch room sounded heavenly.

We rounded the corner to the hall her room was in.

She unlocked the door with a key she had on a necklace. She took a look up and down the hall, keeping an eye out, and then motioned for me to enter first.

That would be just my luck to have the third looper suddenly pop up when we were so close. I was glad Ms. Blithe had my back.

It was dark inside, but even when my eyes had adjusted, they still didn't process what I was seeing.

All the tables and chairs had been moved to the sides of the room haphazardly.

All but one chair.

There was rope in loose circles around the legs.

"Ms. Blithe?" I asked, turning to face her.

But I felt a hard *crunch* as something crashed into the back of my head.

The whole room went black.

CHAPTER 34

I came to awhile later, my head was screaming with pain. I had also drooled even more down the front of my shirt. *What was my deal?*

That's when I noticed I couldn't move my arms or legs. I dreamily looked around at myself.

I had been tied to the chair with the very rope I had seen!

I squirmed, trying to somehow wiggle free, but I could tell it was pointless. I saw a figure leaning on Ms. Blithe's desk.

Could this be the third looper? Did they somehow subdue her, and then me? I looked around. It was only myself that was tied up. That's when it finally started to sink in.

"I'm sorry I have to do this, Freddy..." the figure spoke.

It was Ms. Blithe. How could I have been so blind?

She stood up and walked closer to me. Her eyes were wide and scary, and they quickly darted around the room

All I could do was stare up at her. The back of my head felt like it was much flatter than it had been this morning.

This was as close as I ever wanted to be becoming *Flat Freddy.*

"You're probably wondering what is going on," she continued, pacing around the room. "I lied to you before."

That was a no-brainer. I tried to laugh, but it made my head ache. Hopefully I wasn't going to be a no-brainer, either.

"Shh, shh, shh," Ms. Blithe cooed. She put a hand on my shoulder. It made my skin crawl in that moment. "You have had a severe knock to the head, you might even be concussed."

A low groan escaped from my mouth. I was slowly starting to work the muscles in my mouth again.

"You have to promise me something, Freddy," Ms. Blithe said. "If this doesn't work, and I see you again tomorrow, please don't hold it against me."

My eyes grew wide in terror. The minimal light in the room made the metallic item in her hand shine.

It was a knife...

CHAPTER 35

Ms. Blithe tried to hide the weapon behind her leg, but I had already seen it. I tried desperately to move in the chair I was stuck in, but I made no progress other than to scoot it a little to the left.

"Don't be scared–that's what *he* told me last time," she whispered, drawing in closer.

"W–who?" I asked. My mouth was numb, and wrestling my tongue was no easy feat. This felt like a whole hive of bees had, until recently, been living in my mouth!

Ms. Blithe looked down at me and blinked. I could see behind her eyes she was back *somewhere* else when she spoke.

"Mr. Harrison," she spat the words out. "He was the one who was going to help me, Freddy, and he lied. He tried to strangle me, I couldn't breathe. He wanted to kill me, Freddy! He destroyed my painting."

She drew in closer, brandishing the knife at me now.

"I got the better of him. I was able to stop him, hurt him back."

"Is that what ended the loop?" I asked, my words were still a little slurred.

"Yes." She paused and thought silently for a moment to herself. "It had to. I had to stop him. I had to. And now I have to stop *you*, Freddy"

Ms. Blithe raised the knife in the air.

Another second, and I would be done for.

However, there was a knock at the door.

CHAPTER 36

We *both* turned.

The person on the other side of the door knocked again.

Ms. Blithe stood frozen above me. It took my brain a moment to register, but once it caught up, I yelled—*loudly*.

"*HELP!*" I cried out.

Ms. Blithe screeched at me, and kicked me hard in the chest. The blow was enough to topple me over. I slammed my head onto

174

the tile floor, and my eyes unfocused again. The noise she made was the same from the hallway when I had been chased.

Ms. Blithe towered over me. She looked even crazier in this moment. She resumed her pose with the knife above me. She was mentally preparing herself as she closed her eyes.

FWOOM!

The art room door suddenly shot open with such force, it collided and stuck into the drywall.

Ms. Blithe turned, but was too slow. Whoever it was had reached her, and threw her off me, into the corner of the room.

There was a sick *snap* as her face connected with the desk and a metallic pang as the knife skittered across the floor.

I turned towards the person who had just saved me.

I couldn't believe it.

"You see, if you only had more muscle on you, you could break out of these ropes, no problem," Coach G mocked me.

CHAPTER 37

Coach grabbed me by the front of the ropes, and hoisted me back up into a sitting position. With one fast movement, he was able to untie the bind, freeing me.

It felt nice to move my upper body again.

I still stared hard at him. I couldn't believe it. Coach should not have been on this side of the school in the afternoon, yet here he was!

"You okay, Freddy?" He asked. Coach knelt down to look me over. His reaction didn't give me the most hope.

"No, but better than I would have been if you didn't show up," I muttered.

This made him laugh. I don't think I had actually seen Coach *laugh* before. His smile in that moment struck me as familiar somehow. I couldn't place it.

"Can you walk?" He asked.

I tried; my legs seemed to still be in good shape.

"I think–watch out!" I cried.

My expression lit up in Coach's sunglasses reflection. He turned around, but it was too late.

Ms. Blithe had run up, and swung down one of her sculptures over his head. It shattered into thousands of pieces.

Coach made a move to grab at her, but his words slurred, and then he toppled over.

Ms. Blithe stood triumphantly over him, and then remembered I was there.

"Where were we, Freddy?"

CHAPTER 38

I wasn't sure there was anything I could do for Coach. His movements had slowed, and he was still doubled over on the ground, groaning with pain.

Ms. Blithe looked back down. Behind her, under a stack of chairs, was the knife. She moved to grab it.

That's when I saw my chance—I just hoped my legs wouldn't fail me now.

I darted from the room. The room door

was a lucky break, still being stuck wide open. I tore down the hallway. I could hear Ms. Blithe's footfalls behind me, too close for comfort.

"Help! Help!" I yelled. I tried to open a few doors, but found them empty.

Where was everyone?

Ms. Blithe rounded the corner behind me. She could move just as fast as a fifth grader!

I looked into Mrs. Teagan's room and saw it, too, was empty.

The assembly!

That must have been where everyone was now!

I didn't dare look behind me. I had to move!

With the most speed I had ever mustered, I cleared the rest of the school en route to the gym.

I was finally putting some distance between myself and Ms. Blithe when I ran past one of the many red fire alarms, and had an idea.

Stopping only for a moment, I pulled down hard on the handle.

Covering my fingers in seconds, ink shot down, turning them with black.

However, nothing else happened.

No lights, no alarm. Nothing.

All I had were wet, black finger tips to show for it.

"Can't have you doing *that* again, Freddy." Her voice called out to me.

She stood at the end of the hallway. The knife was clutched firmly in her hand.

I didn't know how, but she had disabled the alarms.

I could hear voices coming from the end of the hallway.

The whole school was still in the assembly, I could still reach them!

As soon as the thought flashed through my mind, Ms. Blithe charged at me again. She screamed the high pitched wail and slashed through the air with her weapon.

I took off towards the gym. I was almost out of danger, all I had to do was get inside!

I grabbed the metal handles of the gym doors and pulled.

But it didn't budge.

I yanked with all my might.

No good.

The doors were locked.

Ms. Blithe rounded the corner down the hall.

She screamed again.

I was trapped.

——— CHAPTER 39 ———

There was nowhere to go.

The only doors opposite were to the lunch room.

The lunch room! That was it.

I tried those doors, and they opened thankfully.

The cafeteria was dark, but I could hear the microphone voice of Principal Ong easily now. The stage that split both the lunch room and the gym only had the curtains to divide it.

I crossed the room, stubbing my shin on a chair I didn't see. It hurt badly and almost sent me toppling off course.

But I had to keep moving!

I heard the lunch room doors bang open behind me just as I had jumped and slid on stage. The curtains dropped over me.

"Freddy..." I heard her voice call out. The lights in the lunch room flickered on, and I could see the other side of the curtains was much brighter now. It wouldn't take long to see the room was empty. I moved backwards, and the curtain caught with me.

As I stumbled out of it, I landed hard on the stage.

Ms. Blithe's footsteps shifted course towards me.

I had to get up and off of the stage before she found me!

The stage floor was covered with miscellaneous set pieces, such as the miniature castle towers you could walk up the back of, and a log cabin stretch of wall that I almost crashed into, despite having navigated this stage a handful of times already.

183

Ahead I saw a billowing wall of curtains that separated the stage from the gym.

Principal Ong was right on the other side!

Ms. Blithe jumped out and slashed at me through the air with her knife. I stopped suddenly, rolling my ankle in the process.

"No—whoa!" I yelled out.

On the other side, I heard Principal Ong stumble in his speech when I yelled. I darted back the way I came, and saw a ladder leading up to the catwalks above.

"Is someone back there?" His voice echoed out.

I threw myself up the ladder, taking rungs two at a time.

"Yes, help me!" I screamed, reaching the top.

Ms. Blithe was right behind me now!

The catwalks swayed underneath as I ran across them. I feared now more than ever the rigging that kept them strapped to the ceiling would give way, and I would come crashing down.

Thankfully, they didn't.

They did, however, end abruptly by the

end of one of the black curtains.

I heard underneath people trying to part the curtains, and a voice yell out, "Where's the button?" Someone hit the button!"

Ms. Blithe had reached the top too, and swung on the first catwalk racing towards me. There was nowhere to go this time.

The mechanical whirl of the curtains being pulled open buzzed loudly in my ear. I turned back to the dead-end and saw the curtains beginning to part—each set sliding automatically across the track.

I was done for, unless I did something crazy myself.

I jumped.

I reached my hands out and found the silk surface of the curtains. Gripping hard, I was moving across the stage as the curtains opened up.

The force of me pulling down on the curtains dislodged a large light above. It came sailing downward, just like the scoreboard had, and exploded onto the stage floor, sending glass and an electrical spark shooting out.

Many teachers jumped out of the way, but

the exposed wire slammed into the curtain and caught fire immediately. It raced up toward me.

I heard another feral scream as Ms. Blithe jumped behind me as well.

She landed so hard underneath, I almost lost my grip.

"FREDDY!" She bellowed, climbing up the curtains.

The fire licked at her own feet. The two were racing to catch me now.

I looked up and didn't see much room for me to go.

Faculty members poured onto the stage, and in turn looked upwards to see us dangling fifty feet up. The others were busy trying to put out the fire.

Ms. Blithe was closing the distance to me.

"Why are you doing this?" I cried out.

"I was able to leave the loop, I *need* to leave the loop! You'll leave the loop, *let me stop the loop!*"

I had climbed up to the top of the curtains. There was nowhere else I could escape to. Ms. Blithe kept climbing with incredible strength.

Unless I did *something*, she was going to get me, or worse yet, the fire would get us *both!*

I have had many dumb thoughts over the years, but this was probably my stupidest idea.

I let go.

CHAPTER 40

Ms. Blithe didn't expect this, and she howled with rage as I crashed into her. I tried to re-grab onto the curtains, but it slipped out of my hands. The ink of my fingers made it slippery, and together we both fell.

This was nothing like falling through the front door earlier. I could see the floor rushing towards us. Our bodies crumpled to the ground, but I had a slightly cushioned fall.

I had fallen on top of Ms. Blithe.

Her eyes were wide and glassy. She kept opening and shutting her mouth, but no words came. Her hands tried reaching out to me, even as she lost more and more of her strength.

The fire had eaten up most of the stage now, and pieces of it were falling down in fiery clumps.

Everyone rushed to us both, and that's when I saw the knife she had in her hands, now plunged into her side. I'm glad it didn't end up in me.

Although, I felt as if I had broken *every* bone in my body.

This was the worst.

Then, Mrs. Teagan was above me.

"Don't move, Freddy! It's all okay! What happened?" Her voice squeaked.

"Please, Coach G is in the art room. He needs help." Was all I could say.

My lungs felt dry, and I coughed several times.

The last face I saw before I closed my eyes was Lauren's.

It was running with tears.

——CHAPTER 41——

I was floating in darkness for a long time. This must have been what it felt like to die. Except I could still hear people around me talking.

This went on for awhile

I felt weak and tired, as if I wanted to sleep for a very long time. My eyelids grew heavy. I was falling, falling—more and more.

I wanted all the pain to stop. I wanted it all to just *end*.

That's when I heard the ring of a bell.

It grew louder and louder.

It became so loud, it felt like it split my head into two.

Everything came back into focus.

I blinked.

I was back in Mrs. Teagan's class.

Last day of school, 9:55 a.m.

I was looping. *Again.*

"Dude, I think..." Dean started to say, but I turned to him.

My eyes were gushing out tears. I couldn't help it.

"Are you okay, Freddy?"

I could feel the eyes of all my classmates on me.

"Mr. Shiner...?" Mrs. Teagan spoke, but she, too, was at a loss.

I ran from the room. I couldn't stop my crying.

I was going to keep looping forever.

I retreated to the one place I knew I could get some privacy—the boy's bathroom.

Thankfully, no one was in the hall to see the waterworks continue. But, I didn't make it to the bathroom.

I stopped outside of the art room. My initial meltdown seemed to fade away when I saw the lights in the room were on. I also heard voices coming from inside.

My curiosity always got the better of me. I opened the door slowly.

Inside, many first graders were running around. On the tables were several boxes of markers, which they all shared to create on their sheets of paper.

The sight confused me, having seen this room for many days now in a row, previously always abandoned and dark. Another sight confused me even more.

Ms. Blithe.

The bags under her eyes were gone. Her hair looked pristine and freshly washed. Her smile was something I realized I hadn't seen for so long. This didn't even look like the same woman I had been around for the past month.

She looked up from a table and saw me. My eyes must have still been red, or she just knew as a teacher something was wrong. She stood up, and swiftly made her way to the door, complimenting a drawing a small red-haired boy held up to show her.

Ms. Blithe ushered me out and shut the door behind her.

"Freddy, what's going on?" She asked.

I took a step instinctively back from her.

"You—you—you said you would help me," I sheepishly said.

Ms. Blithe frowned. "Freddy, is this about your drawings? I thought we had made a lot of progress this year."

I stared at her, flabbergasted. Was this a ploy to try and trick me into feeling safe again? No—she didn't seem to be *anything* like the Ms. Blithe I had been looping with.

But how?

She continued. "Freddy, I know going to a new school can be scary. But, you can't stay here forever. You're going to look back on your time here and be happy that it put you on the right track."

Ms. Blithe then moved towards me and wrapped me up into a big hug. It happened so quickly I didn't have time to protest, and I'm glad I didn't.

I cried, and she held me there.
Ms. Blithe, the real one, was back.
But I was once again all alone.

CHAPTER 42

The hallway clocks let out their digital chimes.
I let Ms. Blithe finally go back into her room
to round up her class.

I knew I could come back and see her again
and again, but in that moment it felt like I was
saying goodbye to her for good.

I made my way back down the halls to find
Lauren standing near my locker. She had my
math book in her hands. She perked up when
I drew closer.

"Freddy, hey, I grabbed this for you," she held it out.

I thanked her and dumped it into my locker. She stared at me.

"Is everything okay?" She asked.

"Yeah," I lied. "Everything is good."

Lauren looked like she wanted to say more, but I felt a hand on my shoulder.

I turned around to see Coach G.

He was alright! I was so glad to see him walking around as if nothing had happened—just like Vic had done.

"We need to talk," he whispered.

I followed Coach. My mind suddenly had a bunch of questions when he asked: "So, how many times have you *looped* so far?"

I stopped in my tracks and glared at him with wide eyes.

"*You*—how do *you* know?" I asked.

"All of the best of us do," he said, and pointed to the display case we had stopped near.

I looked at the names again.

Was he telling me all these kids went through what I did, too?

"It's funny though, every one that I knew of looped their first days. Yet, here we are on the last day," he looked around at the bare hallway. "It was probably my favorite of the loops so far."

So far?

"What do you mean, *so far?*" I demanded.

"Last days of school are bittersweet. You look at all the time you spent over the year, and in one day, it's gone. Over. Done. Teachers can feel the same way, Freddy. I wanted to help anyone else who might have gone through what I did when it was their time. I had no idea your art teacher was also looping. I'm sorry I didn't help in time."

"So wait, you were looping too? Why didn't you say anything?" I asked.

"It's not my business to. I could tell you what I know, but to each one of us," he looked back to the case, "it's personal."

I didn't know what to make of this.

"What about Ms. Blithe?"

He laughed.

LAUGHED!

"She's just fine. You helped end her loop,

but she'll never know. All the time she spent in this loop is gone forever now. What a waste, if you ask me!"

He grew serious again. "But, that's not the way for *you* to end your loop. Can you honestly say the *you* before today was the better version of you?"

I thought about it, but I didn't have to for long. I thought of my friends, talking to Lauren, even reading some of those books I would have never *touched* as the me before today.

"See?" Coach joked with me. "Why else do you think I made you run all those laps? I wanted you to be the better you when you finish your loop."

I stopped him, "Finish my loop? How do I do that?"

Coach stood back up straight and placed his hands on his hips.

"The loop will end when you are ready for it to end. Just take another look at these kids. Each one started their year as someone else, and on the other side of their loops, became the people they *wanted* to be."

Coach pointed a finger to one of the

plaques in the middle of the case.

Gerold Dunn: Pie Eating Contest Winner. Grade 4.

"This was before my loop, before I found out how much I could love working out," he said.

I looked at the photo again of the kid smiling. It was the same smile he still had today. When he *did* smile, of course.

"But, if anything, it just shows you I was a winner *before* I found myself."

I think I was the only kid at Briarwood Elementary to ever discover what the 'G' stood for in Coach's name.

——CHAPTER 43——

I aced my history test that day.

It wasn't hard at all, really. Vic still looked shocked.

I ignored the three of them for the rest of the day.

Coach let us have an hour of free time. He said something about how he was going to make us do inventory, but he had all the numbers already.

I don't know if I was finally accepting my

fate, but I willingly took a tray up to get the meatloaf for lunch. It looked just as bad as ever. The chunks of meat and something else brown didn't look appetizing in the slightest. Not to mention, the bloody looking sauce.

I was thinking hard about my choice when Vic and Aaron sat down. I drowned out their words, even Dean's when he sat down.

I picked up my fork.

All three of them grew silent.

I scooped up a big chunk of a lighter brown meat, and without hesitation, popped it into my mouth.

I chewed a few times and wanted to cry *again*.

I had gone weeks, maybe *months*, without eating, and the worst part was, this stuff *was* actually good! The darker parts were ground beef, and the lighter was potato. It was absolutely delicious!

Vic joined in, and found once again he really liked the stuff, too!

Aaron wasn't as brave, and Vic and I fought over who would get to split his. I won eventually when Vic excused himself to the garbage can. I didn't even mind him throwing up in the background.

I remembered how happy the lunch lady was when Vic got her recipe, so I did the same. I told her it was the best tasting meal I ever had at school. She and I agreed it needed a better presentation.

I didn't see it, but she smiled as she watched me walk away–perhaps the first smile since working at the school.

We *actually* had art class today.

Ms. Blithe let us treat ourselves to time on our tablets, which I skipped in favor of finishing the paperback book I had only a few chapters left of.

It wasn't part of any reports we had due today, but one I found on the shelf that looked interesting. I was actually able to complete it before the hour was up, *lucky me!*

I also absolutely *hated* it.

I thought for sure the story would have went one way, but it ended up turning into something entirely different by the end.

I could have wrote a better ending!

I started playing around in my head about

how I would have deviated, and made a more satisfying ending. It was actually a lot of fun!

For once in my life, I went an entire art class without doodling.

"To all our departing fifth graders, good luck next year in middle school! You all really lit a fire at this school, and you should all be proud of yourselves!" Our principal spoke into a microphone.

The applause he received was lackluster.

I tried to make up for that by clapping twice as hard.

Other fifth graders turned to glare at me. Even the third grader a few rows ahead was turned around to look at me.

The clock positioned in the gym read 2:30 p.m.

It didn't matter.

I would loop once again.

Maybe tomorrow I could get more information out of Coach on how to end the loop once and for all. I was ready to just go home and sleep.

"Thank you all, please return to your classrooms and have a great summer break!"

We all emptied out our lockers. I scooped out every last paper from the bottom, and made sure it looked nice for the next fifth grader who would get it.

Mrs. Teagan was handing out sheets of paper to everyone. I took one from her as she cleared her throat.

"Well, here we are kids. Another year is gone. I'm going to miss you, but I don't feel half as bad when I know that the middle school teachers will have to deal with you now!" She laughed at her own joke. "In your hands, I want you to write a message to the fifth grader who will get your locker next year."

I looked down at the paper in my hand.

I felt there wasn't enough space on the paper to unload what I wanted to on someone. I thought about it for a moment. I seemed to be the only one taking it seriously. I retrieved a pen out of my backpack and began to write.

I kept it short, but hopefully it would help *someone* in the future.

Or, I was just going to keep writing notes that vanished each and every day.

It didn't seem to bother me as much anymore.

I was done before everyone else, and instead of joining the masses grouping by the door, I saw the same fire alarm handle again. I thought of the dangerous crowd pushing and shoving, and thought:

Why not?

I pulled it down fast to avoid my hand being sprayed with black ink once more, but wasn't fast enough and still got a little inked. The lights on the ceiling spun around this time, and the bell rang early. The kids nearest the front began piling out.

There wasn't as mad of a rush to escape the building as there had been before. In moments, the halls were empty.

I flipped the handle back up. The lights kept going, but at least the noise had stopped. I had to remember to do this again tomorrow. It seemed like fun, especially when I knew there was no way for them to know it was me. Maybe there was a way I could use a pencil or something to create separation. I'd try it tomorrow.

I tucked the guilty hand into my jacket pocket.

"Good thinking," Lauren said behind me.

It made me jump.

"What—huh?" Was all I could say.

She pointed to the fire alarm.

"I could see it getting pretty packed in here, so it was smart thinking to let them out early," she resounded, flashing her smile.

"Well, yeah, don't want anyone getting hurt," I said cooly.

"You're a good guy, Freddy Shiner!" She laughed, walking towards the door. I followed her for as long as I could.

She turned back at the door and faced me.

"Are you alright?"

"I..." I wanted to tell her everything, so why couldn't I? It's not like she would remember. "No—I've been repeating the last day of school over again and again. My art teacher tried to kill me, and the only person I can talk to about any of this, because my friends all think I'm crazy, is Coach G!"

Lauren's face grew slack as I rambled on. But she snapped it back just as quickly, and the usual smile I had grown accustomed to seeing returned.

"That's quite the imagination you've got there, Freddy." She joked, putting her hand on the door bar. "Well, see you this summer, right?"

I blinked. What did she mean by that?

The door opened in front of her, and she disappeared outside. The light caused me to raise a hand in front of my face.

The smell of summer air wafted to my nose.

I blinked again.

Creeping towards the door, I pushed it open.

I found busses, and the carpool lane with happy kids piling into cars. Many were unlatching their bikes and calling out to each other. The cross guard signaled for the traffic to stop with his bright red sign.

I took a step outside.

My foot was on solid ground.

The door shut behind me.

I was *actually* outside!

The sun felt so good on my skin, I wanted

to soak it all up.

Lauren was getting into her mother's car. She turned back and waved at me. I waved back. I must have looked silly with the biggest smile on my face.

Out of everyone here, *I* had to be the one who was looking forward to summer the most. I couldn't wait to get home, I wanted to spend some time writing tonight, too!

A car horn honked, and my eyes started tearing up again.

Dad, Mom *and* Julie were all standing outside our car, waving to me.

I skipped down the stairs three at a time. I couldn't wait to hug them all.

Summer was *finally* here.

Inside the school, the bell rang out again.

Louder.

And louder.

About the Author

Before starting to write books, Squall Charlson previously worked both in front and behind the camera on various movies, television shows, and commercials.

He is currently based out of Kansas City, where he, his wife, and their two cat children (Ralphie & Rambunctious (Rambo for short)) live.

About the Illustrator

Marcelo Biott is an artist/creator who loves dipping his pen into different worlds to create new inspired stories and characters. He is the creator of stories such as *InfraCity* and is the artist for books like *Nook* and *The Neverland*. When invited to be the cover artist of *Terror Valley*, he jumped at the chance.

Marcelo loves horror—mostly when he can view it from behind a blanket!